DEPARTMENT
of
TEMPORAL
ADJUSTMENT

By Veronica R. Tabares

Paperback Edition

Cover layout by Tara Tabares

Sun Break Publishing, Seattle, WA

Published by Sun Break Publishing, 1037 NE 65th St. #164, Seattle, Washington 98115.

ISBN: 978-1-60916-002-9

Publishers note:
This book is a work of fiction and a figment of the author's imagination. Similarities to actual characters, places, names, or events are purely coincidental.

Onny—

We have had some great adventures so far.

Are you ready for more?

DEPARTMENT OF TEMPORAL ADJUSTMENT

Chapter 1

"LEFT!" I YELLED, UNABLE TO keep my voice low. "There's the sign! This is it, turn right here!"

My husband quickly moved into the lane to turn right, and I realized that he must not have heard my directions clearly. I frantically tried to correct his mistake before we had to waste more time turning around yet again.

"No, no, no!" I squeaked, "I said left, turn right here!"

"That's what I'm doing," Tony said through gritted teeth with what appeared to be ultimate patience. "We *are* turning right."

"You're not listening," I said in the calmest voice I could manage. "I said to turn left right here."

3

"I don't think *you* are listening, since that doesn't make the least bit of sense," Tony responded in a voice tinged with frustration. "We can't turn left and right at the same time. Do we need to turn left, or right?" He seemed to be a bit distressed, but I could not figure out what he was getting so upset about. All he had to do was drive the car and follow my directions—nothing complicated about that!

"Left, at this next road coming up...right here!"

"Just point."

I pointed to the left, and Tony swerved into the left-hand lane to make the requested turn.

Finally, we were heading in the right direction. I turned to smile at my husband and realized that in my excitement to get where we needed to go, I had probably handled the whole exchange the wrong way. My poor Tony was the perfect picture of the harassed husband, with his clenched jaw, tense shoulders, and death grip on the steering wheel.

"Sorry, I didn't mean to yell," I admitted contritely. He glanced in my direction and I cringed at the expression on his face. It was clear that my apology had not been accepted, since he was now the picture of the cantankerous cab driver as well as the quintessential harassed husband.

I glanced toward the back of the car to see if my loudness had upset the children, who were being suspiciously quiet, and was relieved to find they had all fallen asleep. At least I was spared the embarrassment of my children witnessing their mother's fall from grace. They, at least, could still think of me as the "calm, cool, and collected" type of person.

"I am just so frustrated," I continued quietly. "Do you realize we have been driving over half an hour, and we still cannot find that stupid road?"

"We'll find it, don't worry," Tony responded, and I was happy to note that his death grip on the wheel had loosened just a bit, and his shoulders had lost some of their tension.

"I hope so."

"How are we doing on time?"

"We still have another half hour before her appointment," I admitted, "but that doesn't take into account that we are supposed to be there fifteen minutes early to fill out paperwork. So in reality we really only have fifteen minutes to find this place."

I turned again to look at the sleeping children in the back seat. This wild goose chase of a drive had come about because my oldest daughter, Becca, struggled with chronic asthma. When I had heard that a neighbor's child had been all but cured by one of the local doctors, I had immediately called to make an appointment for my child.

I had been informed firmly and calmly by the receptionist that the doctor was no longer taking new patients, and that there was a long list of people who were waiting for an opening. The thought of my daughter in the midst of an attack had caused pride to fly out of the window as I had begged and pleaded, and had somehow managed to convince the receptionist to find room for my child.

I knew that it was paramount that we arrived for the appointment on time. If we blew this chance, there was no way any amount of begging and pleading would win a second one. Which was why I had allowed a full hour for a drive that should have only taken about ten minutes.

Should have. Unfortunately, the directions given to me by the office staff had proven to be confusing, unclear, and just plain wrong. Half the streets I had been told to drive past had never materialized, and it seemed that the streets we were supposed to turn onto were elusive enough that I was beginning to suspect they had either been renamed or had never existed at all.

I held on tight as my husband quickly made a right turn at my urging. But somehow, nothing looked quite right. We should have been in the middle of a series of medical offices, and this street could only be termed residential. It only took a few minutes of driving to realize that we must have made another wrong turn.

"Darn it! I must have misread the sign...again," I sighed. "As much as I hate to admit it, I think we might as well give up and go home. We'll never make it to the doctor's on time, and there is no way they'll give us another appointment if we're late to this one. Why *would* they give such bad directions?"

Tony made the block through the residential area and pulled back out onto the main road. He drove for a couple of minutes, looking all around to get his bearings.

Tony was one of those rare people who had the most amazing sense of direction. No matter where he was he could always find his way. Put him in a city he has never seen, tell him where you want to go, and he'd somehow miraculously get you there.

If he were a superhero he'd be Map Man, or the Right Direction, or, or...well, he'd be something that instantly identified him as the man with the infallible inner compass who always knew the way to...well, anywhere.

But every Superman has his Kryptonite, and I'm afraid for my Map Man, it's me. I must have my own personal magnetic field, because I seem to have an amazing talent for confusing directional issues.

Tony, tired of driving around aimlessly, pulled into a half-empty parking lot and turned off the car.

"Okay," my husband said more calmly than I deserved, "tell me again the directions they gave you."

"They said to turn left out of our driveway, and then take another left..."

"Wait, wait, wait! The doctor's office told you to take a left out of our driveway? How did they know that we would need to take a left?"

"Oh, they didn't. I added that part. I knew we'd need to take a left."

"So leave out the part you added, and read to me *exactly* the directions they gave you."

"Well, to be perfectly honest I didn't *exactly* write them down. I mean, you know how people around here say go north until this road, and then go west, or east, or north by southwest. It is so confusing. So when I wrote them down I converted them."

"What does that mean, you converted them?"

"You know, got rid of all that north, south, east, west stuff."

"You converted north, south, east, and west to right, left, and straight?"

"Yes, it was easy. I just remembered that if you face north, east is to your right, south behind you, and west to your left."

My husband closed his eyes for a moment and seemed to be muttering to himself. I could not hear exactly what he was saying, but I'm pretty sure I heard something about the "lack of common sense," "how can someone so smart be so dumb," and "it might be true that blondes are airheads."

I was beginning to get a bit miffed as the mumbling continued for several minutes, but I decided that I should pretend I could not hear him and keep my mouth shut. After all, if Tony put his mind to it he might be able to get us to the appointment on time. I evidently could not. I could only get us more and more lost.

After what seemed an eternity, Tony finally stopped grumbling and pulled himself together. "So," he asked in a voice he probably thought was kindly but I found patronizing, "what is the address again?"

"It's on Fifteenth," I calmly said, looking at my notes. I would keep my cool if it were the last thing I did.

"Is that Fifteenth Avenue or Street?" I could tell that he was trying his hardest to keep his frustration in check.

"Um, I didn't write that down. I only wrote down Fifteenth N."

Tony slammed his hand down on the steering wheel, accidentally honking the horn and startling a pedestrian who just happened to be walking by at that moment. Tony smiled and waved an apology to the pedestrian, and then turned to me.

"Sweetie, I think I know our problem. I know why we couldn't find the streets we're were supposed to find."

I hated it when he called me sweetie in that particular tone of voice. It made me feel that he thought I had the brain of a three year old.

"How could you possibly know why we were having so many problems just by hearing the name of a street?" I challenged. "I mean, we're on Fifteenth right now!"

"Yes, that's true. But we're not on Fifteenth N. We're on Fifteenth NE." His response was smug, as if he knew something that I could not possibly comprehend.

"Fifteenth N, Fifteenth NE, what's the difference. It's the name of the street, Fifteenth that counts, right?"

"Not quite. Fifteenth NE and Fifteenth N are in different parts of town. Fifteenth N is on the other side of the highway. I'm pretty sure it's in Greenwood."

"Greenwood? I just don't get it. How do you know what part of town by the N, S, E, W thing?"

"SW is West Seattle, S is south of downtown, NE is over here near Northgate..." Tony looked at my face and sighed. I must have looked as confused as I felt.

"I'll explain later," he said patting my leg. I hated it when he treated me like a child. "We have to hurry if we want to get Becca to the appointment on time."

I decided to let the "treating me like a child" thing go for now. Tony evidently thought he could still get us to the appointment on time. I'd deal with his attitude later. Maybe. After all, I was the reason we had gotten lost in the first place. Accepting my husband's condescending attitude seemed a fitting punishment for my mistakes.

Tony took a moment to get his surroundings and I could see the exact moment when his internal GPS system kicked in. He must have found a way to block my magnetic field and gotten his compass working again, because Map Man was alive and well and ready to save the day. Amazing!

"If we go this way..." Map Man began, but I grabbed his arm to stop his words.

I had seen a most unusual sight.

"Tony," I whispered, "do you see those men? The ones right over there?"

"Why are you whispering?" Tony whispered back. "No one outside the car can hear you."

"Over there, across the street." I gripped his arm tighter. "Those three men who are dressed like old-timey aviators. They are walking so strangely, like they have steel rods stuck in their back. All three of them. Do you see them?"

"Yeah, I see them. They do look a little strange, but I don't think there's anything to worry about. We're pretty near the U-district. They are probably part of a fraternity prank, or they have to walk around like that because they are being hazed."

"I don't know," I said. I wondered if it would be possible to convey the weird feeling I had about these men to my level-headed husband. "They look somehow beyond U-district strange...they look like, well, like they are straight out of an old sci-fi movie."

"Don't worry about it. Like I said, they are probably trying to join a frat. We need to get moving, or we're going to be late."

And again, the condescending pat on the leg.

Chapter 2

"MOMMY," SCREAMED BECCA AT THE top of her lungs. "I need help!"

I ran from the back of the house where I had been folding clothes, fear coursing through my veins. Images of blood, broken bones, and cracked heads crowded my vision as I tried to determine the direction from which the call had come.

"Please, please, please be okay," I muttered fervently as I thought about the new bunk bed we had bought just a week ago. Becca loved jumping on her bed, but now she slept on the top bunk. If she had tried to bounce from that height...her head would hit the ceiling...Becca would get a concussion...the fall would break bones...could a mother get to her baby in time?

Rushing into my daughter's room, I stopped short in the doorway and breathed a sigh of relief.

Instead of blood and broken bones, I found my oldest daughter sniffling loudly in the middle of her room, totally surrounded by open newspapers. "Becca darling," I questioned, relief tingeing my voice, "what is the matter? Did you fall? Are you hurt?"

Becca looked at me as a fat teardrop escaped from the corner of her eye, rolled down her cheek, and plopped onto a front page headline directly below.

"I . . . I . . . I," stuttered Becca, and then the worried look on my face was too much for her sensitive nerves. She burst into loud, gulping sobs.

I ran over to my daughter and wrapped my arms around her little shaking shoulders.

"It will be okay sweetie, it will be okay. Just tell me what happened."

Had I said the wrong thing? Instead of feeling better, Becca just cried harder.

"Take a deep breath. Look at me, Becca, and do what I do."

I pushed my daughter away slightly and turned her until we were eye to eye. I slowly breathed in and out.

Becca followed my lead and tried to take the calming breath, but was interrupted by several gulping sobs. I kept modeling the calming breath technique until Becca regained some calmness.

"Now sweetie, tell me what is wrong."

"I," began Becca, and then her bottom lip slid forward and began to shake. A sure sign that Becca was about to lose it again.

"Take another deep breath," I ordered. "Just shake your head to answer my questions. Did you fall and get hurt?"

Becca's head moved from side to side in an adamant no. Her lower lip stopped vibrating.

"Okay, good. Now, did one of your sisters get hurt, or did you see someone at school get hurt?"

"No, Mommy," Becca responded, seeming to calm a bit. Her lower lip resumed its normal position and no longer protruded.

"Great! Now, does it have to do with these newspapers spread all over the floor?"

Becca's lower lip immediately jumped back out into the dangerous position, but she managed to nod her head affirmatively.

"Ah, so now we're getting somewhere. Do you have a school project? You know I'll help you, like I always do," I said as I hugged my stressed daughter. School projects were the bane of the household.

"I have to do a poster, where I find a bunch of newspaper stories that all go together. And there are so many! How am I supposed to choose?" Becca's last words were barely understandable, as the tears once again began to flow. Only a mother's experience dealing with tears allowed me to translate the sputters into English.

"No problem, sweetie! Look, here's a trick. Pick one of the headlines. There are sure to be other stories on other days when it makes a headline."

"But which one? How do I choose?"

I looked down at the newspapers spread around the room. My eye was immediately caught by the same word glaring at me from three separate headlines.

"Look, Becca," I said excitedly, snatching up the appropriate newspapers. "Here, and here, and here. Look, all of these headlines are about a new man-made element that is being tested. They are all about the same thing!"

"Really? You mean I can use these and not look any more?"

"Sure, darling. Let's look them over together, just to make sure they are what you want."

"It says here that local scientists feel that this new element may be the answer to any energy crisis we may have in the future. They plan to put it through a battery of tests, and if the tests are successful, they will release their findings to the rest of the world."

Becca looked at me, and tears started to pour out of her eyes again.

"What's the matter darling," I asked, grabbing the munchkin and giving her a big hug.

"It's...it's...it's...,"

"It's what, darling?"

"It's…it's…,"

"Come on sweetie pie, tell me what's wrong?"

"I can't use that story, it's too boring!"

"Too boring? What do you mean it's too boring?"

"If I make a poster with all those big sciencey words, my friends will call me names and think I'm smart. They'll make fun of me."

I sat back on my heels and looked at my daughter. I had encountered similar feelings in my childhood, but not at such an early age. Unlike my daughter, at the ripe old age of eight I was still worry free and unafraid of how my peers might see me or think of me.

Peer pressure seemed to be rearing its ugly head at rather an early age. Was it the region we now lived in? My husband and I had moved here from a different part of the country. Or was it just that my daughter was particularly sensitive?

Whatever the cause, I decided that although I wanted Becca to overcome her feeling that she must conform to the will of the crowd, now would not be the best time. She was entirely too distraught to listen to a lecture.

Besides, anyone who had ever tried to reason with an eight year old knows that it requires a strong will and a clear mind. Right now, I had too much homework cluttering up my brain.

"No problem," I said gently to my little socialite, "let's take another look at the paper and see if we can find any other stories that you like better."

I started scanning the headlines, and looked up at my daughter to see if anything was catching her interest.

The little twerp had grabbed the comics and was sitting cross-legged beside me.

"Beckie-girl, you are supposed to be looking through the paper with me,"

"I am, Mommy."

"No, Becca, we are looking for something that you find interesting."

"But this is interesting, Mommy. Look at this one, it's so funny. See this dog…," her voice trailed off as she realized that I truly was not pleased.

"What's the matter, Mommy? You have a funny look on your face. Does your tummy feel bad? Do you want me to ask Daddy to make you some chamomine tea?"

Chamomine! Chamomine was one of a whole list of words that Becca had somehow never learned to say correctly. Her sisters, being the good little sisters that they were, had copied the speech patterns of their big sister. Now we often heard, "I need a mapkin," or "Can we have skapetti for dinner tonight?"

I could not help myself. I grabbed the little sweetheart and tickled her until all vestiges of worry left her face.

How people manage to be serious or mean to children, I'll never understand. They are so sweet, innocent, and just plain funny!

As Becca's giggles died down, I turned again to the newspaper and was surprised to immediately find the answer to her homework problem.

"Becca, look! It says here that there is a theft ring operating that is stealing all the copper wiring. It seems copper is very expensive, and it is believed that the thieves are selling the copper to scrap yards to make money for drugs."

"That's a good one, Mommy! Everyone knows that drugs are bad for you."

"That's right darling. Now, it looks like there are other stories all about the same thing, the copper being stolen. Do you want to use these articles?"

It was as if the clouds had parted and a bright ray of sun had focused on my daughter. The glorious smile that lit her face was plenty of reward for the little help I had given her. I felt like Super Mommy. I could tell by the expression on my daughter's face that I had saved the day.

Chapter 3

I LOOKED AT MY WATCH and rolled my eyes skyward as I realized I still had hours of work to do. I did not know why I wasted my time rolling my eyes up. There was nothing there except the dingy archaeology lab ceiling. No beautiful sky and no possibility of one for many, many hours.

To be honest with myself, I was not really surprised at the amount of work I had left to do. This class had proven itself to be a perpetual nightmare almost as soon as it had begun.

Most professors are on top of things and have their courses thought out and well designed—but not this one. This professor had evidently seen too many old movies and modeled himself after every absentminded professor ever invented. He had transformed a week's worth of lab work into a painful series of never-ending, ever-shifting deadlines. As soon as one task was complete, the professor discovered another detail that was absolutely essential that had somehow been left out of the instructions. So we lowly students were forced to begin at the beginning and do the whole thing over again.

Or fail the class. Which we all knew was not a real option.

So here I was, stuck in the basement at two o'clock in the morning, nowhere near finished. I still had hours upon hours of drawings to complete.

It was a real problem that this archaeology professor had begun his academic career in Art rather than in archaeology. After I got the first assignment back, I realized that it was not enough to do accurate drawings. No, this professor critiqued the technique and artistic merit of the drawings. There was no possibility of doing an accurate but sloppy job on the drawings and moving on to the next assignment. Unfortunately, I had never taken a single drawing class.

When I first signed up for the class, I had wondered why students were required to check out keys to the lab. Now I understood. The detailed measurements and calculations demanded by the professor took an outrageously long time, and the drawings...well, they required a meticulousness that needed a safe, uncluttered, quiet setting. No distractions.

So I found myself in this stinky old basement instead of at home, where I would not be safe from distractions even in the middle of the night. There had been innumerable times when I had gotten to a crucial part of my calculations, only to be interrupted by a child who fell of a bed, had a nightmare, or needed a drink of water.

The thought of my little munchkins at home, snuggled up in their beds looking like angels, made me smile. It also reminded me that while it was essential that I worked hard to get my degree, the really important people in my life would need me tomorrow.

I calculated the amount of work I had left to do, glanced at my watch once again, and made the difficult decision to go home, finished or not. I did not have classes to attend the next day, but my lovely and rambunctious daughters would be requiring my full attention and loads of energy. I had no intention of short-changing my children just because I had decided to pursue a degree.

As I slid off the tall stool provided by the school for the students' sitting pleasure I realized two things. First, the stool must either be a part of a science experiment gone wrong or it had been created by a sadistic engineer, because the second was that my leg had fallen asleep.

"Not again," I grumbled. It seemed that every time I spent more than three hours on one of those stools some part of my body fell asleep. I could never look forward to buckling down to long hours in the lab because I absolutely hated the tortuous prickly feeling that meant that blood had once again begun to circulate.

My first supposition that this was a part of a science experiment must be the correct one. I wondered where they hid the camera. It was certain that someone was at this moment documenting my reaction to this uncomfortable situation. It felt like an invisible being was using me as a pincushion. Or, to be more accurate, multiple invisible beings, thousands of invisible beings, each with their own very sharp, very hard, very long needle.

Cautiously I stretched my arms over my head, testing other parts of my body to see what might have decided to take a nap. My achy muscles reinforced the decision to call it a night. My neck was extremely sore from bending at just the right angle to see the shard, and my hands were beginning to cramp from holding the pencil for so long.

I had to learn how to take breaks more often. Finishing this project was not worth my body becoming twisted like a pretzel.

Although I must admit that going home looking like a pretzel would have one benefit. My children would think it was hilarious. There would be amusement value.

I gathered my purse, double-checked that my keys were firmly in my hand, and reached deeper into my bag to retrieve the pepper spray my husband had given me for my late-night forays into the lab.

It was only a short walk from the lab to the parking lot where I had parked the car a mere five hours ago, but better safe than sorry.

Moving to the door, purse in hand, I flipped off the light. I reached for the knob but stopped short of turning it. I paused to listen to the strange whirling noise that had caught my attention.

Whatever could it be?

Shrugging my shoulders, I gripped the knob tighter and began to turn. I had just opened the door a crack when my movements were halted once again, but this time by what I saw.

It was the freaks! The same ones my husband and I had noticed the day before.

What were they doing in the archaeology building, and why were they coming out of the janitor's closet?

Carefully and quietly I closed the lab door. Another ten minutes in the lab would not hurt me. Surely that crowd would not stay around this almost deserted building any longer than that.

Besides, what was ten minutes, or even an hour for that matter? The important thing was that I avoided whatever mischief that freaky crowd had planned.

Chapter 4

"OKAY DARLING, I'LL BE RIGHT home. My bus should be here any moment," I whispered into my cell phone. "Yes, I know you hate it, but let them do it anyway. No, don't worry—I'll take care of it when I get home."

I glanced at my fellow bus stop inhabitants, and I was relieved to see that not one of them had any interest in my purely domestic conversation.

"I said I'll take care of it when I get home," I said louder, since it was evident from his responses that my husband was having trouble hearing me. "But I understand what you are saying."

"Listen darling, just don't worry about it, I'll clean it up when I get home." Tony was still having trouble hearing me, so I raised my voice a bit more. I looked around at those waiting for the bus with me. I might as well have been alone in the middle of a desert for all the attention I was getting.

I took several steps away from the group onto a grassy area. It had rained recently so it was muddier, but that meant it was also more private. I felt that there was now enough distance between me and everyone else that I could raise my voice to a normal level. My husband seemed to not be able to hear me properly when I spoke in a lowered voice.

I listened to the sound of my husband's voice for a few minutes and realized that he still had not heard me properly.

"Tony, don't worry," I said calmly, but more loudly, "it's good for them."

"Of course not," I responded. Could he still not hear me?

"No, it won't teach them to be slobs! Just let them do it, okay."

I felt eyes on me the moment frustration crept into my raised voice. I looked up to see every person at the bus stop looking my way.

How embarrassing.

For years I'd fought the degradation of good manners fostered by the cell phone culture. The overly loud voices, the embarrassing secrets not kept secret. The number of conversations I'd heard in public places that should have remained private...the number my children had heard!

After one particularly embarrassing bus ride, during which I could not escape from one side of an R-rated conversation, I decided that I would rather die than become one of those rude, obnoxious people who carried on loud, private cell phone conversations in public places. I vowed that all my conversations would remain low-key, low-voiced, and G-rated.

Based on quite a few faces, I had piqued the interest of my fellow travelers. But since my conversation contained nothing vulgar or private, it must have been my tone.

"Fine," I said in a once again lowered voice, "but remember what I said...it's good for them. I've got to go now—my bus is turning the corner. I'll be home in a few minutes."

I smiled as I closed my phone and stuck it in my purse. All this fuss about such a little thing! My husband absolutely hated messes, and it disturbed him when the kids used sheets and blankets to make a fort in the living room.

My theory was that living-room-fort-building was a win-win situation. The kids had a blast using their imaginations, they had a nice dry place to play on a rainy day, no one got hurt, and all we had to do was fold the linen again and the room was as good as new.

I still could not figure out why such a harmless activity bothered my husband so much.

Just as my bus pulled up to the stop a group of men came down the hill and streamed between the bus and the passengers waiting to board.

An odder group I truly have never seen. There were about fifteen of them, and they seemed to have walked off of a 1950s movie set—with their slicked-down, side-parted, long side-burned hair, black slacks with black shoes, plaid or white shirts, and pen protectors sticking out of the front pocket of every one of their shirts.

Even their skin seemed odd. It was somehow too smooth, too blemish-free...too perfect to be true. I've only seen that kind of perfection with the aid of makeup, which confirmed my movie set theory.

The group finally cleared the bus, and I watched their progress down the hill as I waited for my turn to board. The group ignored everyone around them as if no one else existed, or as if everyone else was too lowly for their notice.

I watched as they reached the street and continued across as a group even though the light was against them. They did not talk together; they just walked in concert as a mass.

As I heard the screech of tires, thankfully not followed by the sound of metal hitting a human body, I knew my guess must be right. Only actors too full of their own importance could be so inconsiderate as to stop the flow of traffic on a busy street.

It was not the first time actors had invaded campus. A movie studio must be using the university grounds as a setting for a 1950s movie.

Chapter 5

I YAWNED, AND NOT FOR the first time—or
even the tenth.

This project was taking *forever* to finish...for
me, at least. My well-rested and unencumbered
classmates had stayed for a mere two hours after
class and had zipped right through the work they
needed to do.

I, on the other hand, was destined to spend
quite a few more hours all alone in the pseudo
comfort of the basement lab of Denny Hall.

The problem was that I was neither well
rested nor unencumbered, which had resulted in a
concerning and irritating series of mistakes. I
simply could not get my brain to achieve the level
of concentration a project of this sort required.

Zoe had run a fever several days this week,
and I could not help but be concerned. She was so

tiny, so fragile, and looked dismally pathetic with her flushed face and lack of energy. To make matters more alarming, she would not eat anything and I had to force her to drink.

My head told me it was nothing serious, that this was a normal part of being a kid. This illness would pass just as Zoe's fear of riding in cars had passed.

But my heart was of the worrier breed and had a different, much scarier opinion. It pulled out a huge spotlight and focused it on every single news report I had ever heard over the years that told about some poor family who had discovered that their precious child had a rare and fatal disease. Then, to make sure I got the point that life could be scary, it spotlighted every known instance reported where a disease was not fatal, but serious enough to change the life of a child forever.

It was not easy to do my schoolwork while my brain and my heart continued to battle. To say it was distracting was an understatement of the monumental sort. Particularly since all I could really do for my child at this time was to console and entertain.

Caring for a sick child—let me tell you—was a huge, exhausting, and horrible job. Walking an ill three year old around the living room for hours at a time was great for building muscles and burning calories, but not much else.

One problem was that I could not use the time to plan what I needed to do, or even think about my assignment, since my children had an innate talent for discerning the exact moment when my mind had begun to wander. As soon as my focus was not entirely on the little angel there would be a pitiful whimper, an uncomfortable wiggle, or occasionally a scream of pain.

Yes, in my house a sick child claimed all brain power available, and left none for silly things like schoolwork.

Now, even though Zoe was over her fever and was feeling better, there was still a twinge of worry. Just enough to distract me from the things I needed to accomplish so I could graduate...so I could help provide a better life for my children...so they could grow up to have children of their own...so they could be tortured by their own kids!

One of my main worries was that my family was not clear of this illness yet. Maybe—if I were very unlucky—a random germ had escaped my massive disinfection effort and the rogue germ was at this very moment stalking one of Zoe's older sisters. If that were the case I would have to begin the whole process all over again. It made me tired just thinking about it!

I often theorized that among every group of germs there were extraordinary ones that were armed with special armor that protected them from disinfectant. They were the Special Forces of the germ world. Their purpose was to survive no matter what, so that they would have the opportunity to infect again.

My theory was first crafted a few months after the birth of my second child, and was validated before my third child had her first birthday. I was so sure that my theory was correct that I had contemplated writing a paper on it. It certainly was a fact that in my household, if one girl got sick, a week or two later the others came down with the same illness no matter how hard I tried to keep the girls separate and immerse everything in disinfectant.

It was imperative that I stopped that rogue germ before it struck! Two weeks from now was mid-terms, an extremely bad time to be distracted, worried, and exhausted. Zoe's older siblings must not get sick!

I yawned again, for what must have been the hundredth time, which prompted me to take a peek at the clock on the wall. Yikes! I'd just wasted a full half hour worrying about a child who was probably happily snoring in her bed and anticipating a situation that might not even happen. If I was lucky.

I must focus! I had no hope of getting all this work completed if I spent all my time day-dreaming. Or should I call it night-dreaming, since it was the middle of the night? But night-dreaming sounded too much like normal dreaming that happened while a person slept. So maybe I should call it awake-dreaming.

"Awake-dreaming," I whispered aloud, trying it out. "Yes, that is much better, since awake-dreaming pretty much sums it up, no matter the time of day."

But as I said the word 'time' aloud, I was shocked out of my awake-dreams. That nasty word, time, was the bane of my existence, the commodity I seemed to be unable to not waste.

I glanced down at the pile of paper in front of me and groaned as I noticed the pen clutched in my hand.

I closed my eyes a second and took a deep breath. I would not panic. I would keep my cool.

But really, I was probably worried unnecessarily. I was a reasonably intelligent human being. I had full control of myself. Why was I worried?

But no matter how much I tried to reason with myself, I was afraid to look at my papers. You see, some people sleepwalk, I awake-dream doodle. The more distracted I was, the more I doodled. And I had been very, very distracted.

I gathered my courage and took a good look. I could not help but groan again, since my entire paper was covered with little squiggles wearing breast-plates and helmets. While I was distracted, my hand had drawn the very germs that had invaded my thoughts.

"Darn it! These squiggles don't look anything like the pottery shard I'm supposed to be drawing. The professor will think I've gone nuts if I turn this in to her. I've got to focus if I ever want to complete this assignment.

"No matter what, I will finish today—even if I have to stay up all night. This is due Friday, so I have no more time to waste.

"I should be able to do it. Tony has the kids safe and sound, and no one ran a fever today. I cannot worry about my family. All is well on the home front.

"I'll sleep all I want later. And after I sleep, I'm sure I'll stop talking to myself.

"Oh, sleep! What a lovely word, sleep. I wonder who first said that wonderful, wonderful word—sleep? Was it a mother, trying to get a cranky child to rest? Oh, there's another great word, rest, and then there is slumber, snooze, doze, nap. So many words for something so simple, something I could do right now if I just let myself relax just a little. And there's another one, relax."

The pain of my head hitting the cold hard table shocked me awake. I hoped it would not leave a bruise, but really, it served me right. How *could* I fall asleep sitting up? I needed to finish my work so I could go home. I needed to stop getting distracted by whatever nonsense was floating around my head. I need to focus.

"It is time you got down to business," I told myself firmly. "Now that you've had a nice little nap, a little deep breathing should clear your head."

I breathed in and out deeply several times to give my body the oxygen it needed to stay alert.

Unfortunately, I soon found myself struggling to stifle a monstrous yawn.

"Not good enough! I need to be more alert than this. It may not require a tremendous amount of concentration, but I certainly can't do it in my sleep. I will finish this, and I will finish it now. I will be awake, alert, and conscious."

I shook my head like a wet dog and stretched my arms over my head. It was lovely to feel the blood once again begin to circulate. Just to make sure everything was working correctly I popped my knuckles. My mother had always told me that popping my knuckles would cause them to swell up like balloons, but it had not happened yet, and if it helped me stay focused...

I had been told by one of the other students that several pieces of the pottery shards were etched with a phosphorescent material. It was a detail that I wanted to include in my findings, but of course, it could only be seen in the dark.

"Well, this is as good a time as any to see this phenomenon," I said to myself decisively. "Off with the lights, and watch for the glow."

I crossed the room, switched off the lights, and turned to walk back to my station.

"Darn it," I said in frustration. "Of all nights to have a full moon, why does it have to happen when I want to look for the phosphorescent etchings! I won't see anything with that lunar spotlight shining in the window. I'll have to close the shades."

I crossed over to the window, but as I reached for the shade my hand was arrested as my

39

attention was caught by a strange humming noise. It was an insignificant noise, not loud at all. If the normal noises of the day had been around, I probably would not have noticed it.

I shrugged my shoulders as I pulled down the first of the shades. The noise was just another distraction, and I would just ignore it. I turned to look toward my work station to assure myself that I was getting the proper result. I smiled as I saw that much of the moonlight that was illuminating my station had already been blocked.

Should I pull all the shades? Probably not, since I had started on the side that shaded my lab station. If I could avoid working in total darkness in this creepy basement I would.

Pulling down two more shades, I turned to again check my work station. Perfect! I was just about to make my way across the dark room when the bright moon projected the moving shadow of a person through a window with the shade still raised. As soon as that shadow passed, another took its place.

"Who could be here this time of night," I whispered to myself. "I hope it is just a couple of security guards patrolling."

I peered around the edge of the nearest shade. I vowed to be cautious, since I did not want whoever was out there to know I was in the basement alone. I was sure it would not be wise.

"Oh, my goodness," I whispered, unsure if I should be more shocked or afraid.

In the bright moonlight, a veritable pageant of freaks poured past the basement window. The group consisted of about fifteen to twenty people, and the moon provided sufficient light so that I could get a good look.

Something was not right. Among the group parading by I recognized both the aviators I had spotted in the U district weeks ago and the 1950s self-centered geeks from the day before.

One thing was certain—even if they were a part of a movie company, they had no business on campus in the middle of the night.

I pulled out my cell phone and called security. I no longer felt even remotely safe in the basement of Denny Hall, not with these freaks and geeks free to roam around all night.

Chapter 6

"DO YOU WANT US TO escort you to your car?" the security guard questioned gently.

I looked at him and smiled. Here was a man who was perfect for his chosen profession. He was kind, polite, and there was real intelligence shining from his soft blown eyes. In my opinion he was the perfect security guard. You could not help but feel safe in his presence. Not only did he have a nice fatherly face, but he was big enough that any football coach would have been crazy not to have recruited him for the high school team.

"Yeah lady, if you feel scared we can take you to your car," the second security guard chimed in.

My gaze shifted to the smaller man, and I had to fight to keep the smile on my face. This man did not engender trust, safety, or calm feelings of any kind.

43

About the kindest feeling I could dredge up when I gazed at his rodent-like visage was sorrow that the poor man had to go through life at such a disadvantage. Not only was he puny, but his resemblance to the rat family certainly did not instill trust—or tolerance.

The more I thought about it, the more I knew I should feel sorry for this guy. He must have been the last person chosen for the team at every playground game as well as the last boy left standing at dances.

I had no clue as to his background, but this puny little man exuded guile and dishonesty. He gave off weird, creepy vibes that warned everyone in the vicinity that they had better beware, a predator was near.

If I spotted this guy following me down the street, with his squinty eyes and shifty look, I would find a safe haven as quickly as possible, all the while hugging my purse tightly to my side.

These uncharitable thoughts flooded my mind for a full two seconds before my better self regained control.

Who was I to pass judgment on this weasel-like little guy? And purely on his looks alone. For all I knew he might not have a vile bone in his body. He might have dedicated his life to helping others feel safe and secure as they go about their campus life. He may spend his time taking care of his ailing mother, entertaining sick children at hospitals, and donating regularly to the food bank.

He may be a veritable saint hidden in the skin of a sad sinner.

I needed to focus on what ultimately mattered—that security was here when I needed them. They had responded immediately to my phone call, and they were thorough enough to start by validating my right to be in Denny Hall in the middle of the night. As soon as they were satisfied that I was not an interloper they checked the premises for trespassers. But they had been unable to find any evidence of other people either in the building or near it.

I should have felt glad that whoever had paraded past had not left any damage behind. Instead I felt foolish. I could tell that the guards thought I was spooked by the loneliness of the building. They thought I was afraid of my own shadow. They believed that the group I had seen marching past was just my overactive imagination in hyper-drive.

And maybe they were right. It was, after all, their job to know what was going on around campus in the middle of the night.

"So lady, we need to make our rounds. What's it gonna be? Do you want us to escort you to your car, or can we get on with our work?"

The security guard's squeaky voice interrupted my charitable thoughts about him, and the uncharitable ones came flooding back. He was really an unpleasant and despicable specimen of a human being.

I scrunched up my face in thought. It was now two o'clock, and I still had a lot of lab work to complete. I could take the guards up on their offer to escort me to my car, but that would mean that I would need to stick around again tomorrow night. Or, I could suck it up, stop being a baby, and complete what I needed to complete.

When I thought about it, it was a no-brainer. The group I thought I saw out of the lab window was probably the work of my sleep-deprived, overactive imagination.

"It's okay. I think I'll just stick around here for a few more hours," I replied.

* * *

Two more hours of concentrated work on the never-ending project and I finally had it completed. To say that I was happy to be done did not even hit close to the mark. I was ecstatic, blissful, jubilant, euphoric, and of course, dangerously exhausted. If I did not know that this room would be filled with students in a few hours, I would seriously consider curling up in a corner and taking a long, long nap.

But then again, my husband probably would not appreciate it if I did not show up. Not just because most husbands become worried if their wives stay out all night, but also because I needed to be there to watch the girls in the morning so that he could go to his classes.

Now, while I still had an active brain, was the perfect time to head home. Driving in my sleep was a habit I did not want to acquire.

I gathered my backpack from the corner of the lab, and had just put my papers inside when that annoying humming noise returned.

What could possibly have made that strange noise?

I gave myself a slap on the face, both to wake myself up better and to knock some sense into me.

"Repeat after me," I said aloud. I felt sure that the sound of a human voice, even my own, would help me understand the words better. "It is none of my business. None of my business, do I hear. None...of...my...business!"

Unfortunately, I knew that mysteries were a weakness of mine. I could ignore them when I had a deadline to meet, but I had just finished the project...

I blame it on my early reading material. I was reared on Nancy Drew and Trixie Belden novels, and as I got older I graduated to Agatha Christie and Dorothy Sayers. I could not ignore a strange noise or an unusual sight. I was compelled to investigate. Or, as I found out earlier tonight, call security.

But I had already called security one time tonight, and had been made to feel the fool. Besides, what would I say? There was a strange noise?

The more I thought about it the more I realized that investigating this particular strange noise only made sense. I'd be spending many more hours alone in this basement before I finally attained my degree. Not knowing the source of that strange, whining, humming noise would drive me batty and distract me from my work.

I only had one course of action open to me. I zipped up my backpack, threw my shoulders back, and marched over to the lab door determined to get to the bottom of the mysterious sound.

The cold of the door knob activated the sense that must have fallen asleep sometime during the night while I was completing the project—common sense.

What kind of detective boldly marched out to investigate possible nefarious activity? What could I have been thinking? Were all those hours spent studying the methods of the greatest fictional detectives for naught?

I took a moment to take stock and realize that my heart was pounding madly. The thought of investigating a real mystery had sent adrenaline rushing through my veins.

But I did not need the energy provided by adrenaline, I needed caution. I needed to regain control of myself before I took another step.

I took a deep breath and cautiously let it out. I was pleased to feel my heart rate begin to slow, and that feeling of excitement begin to cool.

After a few more breaths I felt more in control. It would not do to make a lot of noise just as I was about to begin my investigation. It might warn any intruders of my presence. Then I might never find out the source of that strange noise.

I knew I could sneak out of a dark room easier than a lighted one, so I flipped off the light switch. Then I hunched my shoulders forward to get into stealth mode. I was ready to sneak and pry. Spy and investigate.

I slowly turned the handle. I listened for sounds in the hallway. All seemed clear.

I eased the door open excruciatingly slowly, and as soon as I had it open an inch I cautiously looked through the opening. It was completely empty.

I gently swung the door wider until I could squeeze my entire head through. I could now see the entire length of the hallway.

Strangely, I was disappointed. All that caution for nothing. There was no one in sight.

Most disappointing of all was the lack of the humming noise. When had it stopped? I had been concentrating so hard on not being seen or heard that I had not even noticed that it had ceased.

I stepped into the hall and gently closed the door behind me, carefully locking it so that it would be safe from the intruders, if they really existed and chose to return.

It was that exact moment that my body decided that it had had enough. Fatigue hit me and I could not resist a yawn. My brain suddenly felt foggy, and I realized that not only was I very, very tired, but I had not eaten in over ten hours.

No more time to play around with kid games. I'd just walk calmly down the hall, out the door, and straight to my car. It should be safe enough by now. Even crooks were probably asleep this close to dawn.

Everything would have been fine and dandy if the humming had not started up again just as I passed the janitor's closet.

I gritted my teeth in frustration. Was someone playing some sort of cruel joke on me? Was there a camera hidden nearby, waiting to record my reactions? Was there a psychological experiment being perpetrated in the bastions of the archaeology department?

Frankly, right now, I really did not care why the noise existed. Strange noises in the middle of the night no longer interested me in the least. The possibility that the psychology department had invaded archaeology space did not worry me. I was simply too tired to play Nancy Drew.

I had one thing, and one thing only on my mind—my bed. More than anything else in the world right now, I wanted to go home, curl up in my bed, and get some glorious, restful slumber.

Well, maybe there was a second thing on my mind—that stupid noise! I could not help but wonder why that irritating sound was coming from the janitor's closet. I was absolutely positive that no janitor in his right mind was in that closet at this time of night. All the sane little janitors were safe and sound in their own little beds, fast asleep.

So I had to wonder, who or what was in that closet?

I stepped back a pace and took a long, hard look at the closet door.

That was odd. I'd never before noticed the plaque over the door. I knew that every door on campus was labeled with a similar plaque that stated the purpose of the room. But I'd never noticed that this one did not actually mention janitor or facilities or custodial at all.

"DTA?" I muttered to myself. "What could DTA stand for? Maybe something like Dust, Trash, and…and…and what? Appliances? No, that doesn't make any sense."

Okay, so the Nancy Drew syndrome had resurfaced. I felt absolutely compelled to have a little peek inside that mysterious closet.

Just in case the closet was inhabited, I resolved to open the door very slowly and very quietly. If I was successful, whoever was inside the closet should never notice my presence. Or at least that was my hope.

Besides, one little peek could not hurt.

Chapter 7

I GRADUALLY AWOKE WITH THAT uneasy feeling that always followed a vivid but strange dream. I sighed as I realized that this particular dream was being extremely slow to release me from its powerful hypnotic grip. I shook my head from side to side a few times, trying to shake off the unaccountably disturbing feeling engendered by the image of thousands of white rabbits robotically hopping around a huge green field.

From past experience I knew that if I did not eradicate the image before I opened my eyes, it would slink back into my thoughts throughout the rest of the day. So with eyes still closed, I mentally changed the scenario. A convoy of white trucks descended upon the green field, the drivers

53

opened up the back doors, and all the creepy rabbits obediently hopped inside. When the last manic rabbit was safely aboard, the drivers shut their doors and drove off toward the horizon, hopefully never to visit my imagination again.

As the last white truck drove out of sight, a large blue, red, and yellow truck pulled into the meadow. A crew of workmen descended and began to unload huge beams of wood painted white and gold. The workmen quickly assembled the structure, and as they retrieved further items from the truck it became apparent the structure was a beautifully crafted carousel.

To complete the pleasant picture, my husband drove up in our car, and my daughters jumped out of the back seat and excitedly ran to the now completed carousel. My husband helped each girl onto her chosen pony and the ride began, complete with the traditional carousel music. The girls did not even attempt to hide their joy as they laughed and giggled in delight.

Now that was an image I could easily return to throughout the day! It was much more pleasant to visualize my children happily playing rather than robot rabbits marching about the meadow.

Now I could safely open my eyes, and it was about time to. I needed to discover how I had ended up unconscious on the floor. Had I lost my balance as I inched open the door and fallen headfirst into the closet? Had I peeked though the door only to hit my head on a tool that had been hung at a dangerous height?

Or, *gulp*, had someone hit me?

It really bothered me that I could not recall how I had lost consciousness.

I opened my eyes, took one look around and *gulped* again in dismay. This was no closet!

And, horror of horrors, there, in front of me in living color, was my dream of the white rabbits recreated. Only instead of rabbits it was men and women in white lab coats, and instead of a meadow it was a huge lab. And instead of hopping, the people walked—with that same robot-like precision of my dream.

"What is all this? Where the heck am I?" I said aloud, unable to keep my thoughts from spilling out of my mouth.

"It is a little hard to explain," a male voice just behind me answered.

Startled, I jumped up and attempted to twirl around to face the owner of the voice, but at that point I discovered that I had not been lying of the floor as I had supposed, but on a table. I was fortunate that the man had quick reflexes and he was able to catch me before my face slammed into the floor.

"Thanks," I said grudgingly, allowing the man to help me into a standing position. As he released my arm I took a few moments to brush nonexistent dirt from the knees of my pants as I surreptitiously looked him over. Was he the type to knock a woman unconscious in a closet?

He was a dark-haired, clean-cut, intelligent looking man of about forty, average handsomeness, wearing a white lab coat. It was unfortunate that none of these attributes qualified the man as safe or trustworthy. Weirdos could come in many shapes and sizes, and evil could be camouflaged to appear harmless. I needed to make full eye contact to learn what I needed to know. Very few people could keep their true characters from shining out of the "windows of the soul." I'd been in enough customer service jobs that I was pretty good at reading those soul messages and figuring out if someone was trying to hide something.

One look at his kindly eyes told me everything I needed to know. These eyes were honest, compassionate, and intelligent. This man meant me no harm.

"So, I'll ask again. Where am I?"

"As you can see, you are in a lab."

"Right. But what lab? I'm pretty sure I've never been in this lab before, and I thought I'd seen every lab on the UW campus. Am I on campus?"

"Yes...you are on campus, and you are right, you have never been in this lab before."

"Hey, wait a minute, how can you be so sure? How do you know where I have or have not been? What is all this? Are you some kind of spy?"

"No, no, no! Don't be upset. I haven't been spying on you. I know nothing about you."

"You know nothing...then how do you know I've never been here before? How can you be sure? Maybe I have been here before!"

"If you had been here before, I would know. So I know you have not."

"And how can you be so sure? I'll bet you don't spend every moment of your life in this room. I could have visited while you were out."

"Not likely. I would have been told."

Had I misjudged the man? Instead of the nice kindly man I had taken him for, was he some kind of tyrant who instilled fear in all his employees?

The man looked at the expression on my face and decided to expand his answer. "I am always informed when someone from the past steps through the portal into our time."

"From the past?"

"Yes, you are now in what you would call the future."

At those words I began to worry. How could I have misjudged the man? How could I have not seen the spark of craziness that must lie just below the surface? Had I lost my ability to read people? Was I in a crazy man's lab?

I took another long look at the man who was patiently awaiting my response. He looked sane enough; yet, if he believed this was the future, he must be insane. Or maybe he was not truly insane, he was just delusional.

"So, you say this is the future?" I kept my voice calm and gentle, so that I would not irritate the man. It would not be smart to aggravate him if he were indeed unstable.

"Not to me. For me, it's the present. You are just in a future time for you." The man answered calmly, showing no physical signs of stress...or instability. Except, of course, the instability of believing that I had traveled through time.

"Come now," I inquired softly, inadvertently speaking as if I were questioning one of my children about a bad dream she had had, "you don't really believe that, do you?"

"I do indeed." The response was firm and calm.

It scared me that the man seemed perfectly sane, and perfectly serious. He appeared to really believe what he was saying.

"You believe this is the future?" I questioned further, accidently letting a little tension creep into my voice.

"Not for me, only for you."

"So what is now for you is the future for me?"

"Yes, except my now is hundreds of years after your now."

The man was so calm, so sure of himself.

"Fine," I continued, slightly irritated that I could not get the man to show any doubt, "let's say, for the sake of argument, that you are right and this is what to me is the future. So explain to me how I got here?"

"From what I can tell, you just walked through the door."

"Walked through the door..." I was confused. What kind of answer was that!

"You walked through the portal. We have one in the basement of Denny Hall. You just wandered right through it."

"You mean the closet door? The closet door is a time portal?" I did not quite know why, but I was beginning to believe that this crazy man might not be crazy. Maybe it was the compassion shining out of his eyes, or the complete lack of tension in his shoulders. It made me want to trust him, and I usually did not feel the urge to trust lunatics.

"I'm afraid so."

I gulped. Could his story be true? Could I be in the future?

"So now I'm in the future?"

"Your future, yes."

I gulped again. His sincerity was too real. His intelligence too evident. I believed him.

"So what happened when I walked through?"

"You weren't prepared to travel, so you immediately lost consciousness."

"For how long?"

"About five hours or so."

"Five hours!" I yelped, frantically looking around for an exit. "I've got to get back home. My husband will be frantic with worry. Where's the closet door?"

"I hate to tell you," the man said calmly, pulling up a chair and sitting down, "but it's not as easy as just letting you walk back through the door."

"What do you mean?"

"Have a seat."

I located a chair across from the man and sat down. Somehow the act of taking a seat helped me to relax a bit.

"Continue," I said as soon as I was comfortably seated.

"There is a lot of red tape. A lot of reports to be filed. A lot of decisions to be made about your well-being."

"I can take care of my own well-being, thank you very much," I said crossly. "Just do whatever reports you need to and show me the closet door, and I'll get out of your hair."

"I wish it was that easy."

"But it's not?"

"Sorry, it's not."

I looked at the man and could not say a word. His eyes appeared so sad, so compassionate. I imagined that the look he gave me was very like the one a doctor would give a patient who had a terminal illness and only had a few months to live.

"Look," the man continued, "other people before you have found their way to our time. It doesn't happen all that often, but when it does we usually just allow the person to stay in our society.

We've enriched our culture tremendously that way."

He looked at me as if he expected a response, but I had nothing to say.

"It's amazing how quickly people entering our world create lives for themselves. Some of them—"

"I already have a life. I want to go back," I interrupted stubbornly.

"Yes, but here you can—"

"Are you telling me I have to stay? That I will never see my family again?"

"Not quite."

"Then what are you saying?"

"I'm trying to prepare you for the possibility that you won't be going back."

"Well, don't even bother trying. I have to go back! My family needs me."

"I'm sure they do, so just calm down. There is no reason for you to get upset before any decisions have been made. There is still research to do, and there have been one or two instances that I know of when someone was returned to their own time after wandering into ours."

"I had better be one of one or two times. I have three kids and a husband. I need to help my kids grow up."

"Just relax for a bit, and I'll check on the research group. They should be done soon."

As the man moved down the maze of pathways toward another part of the lab, I began to worry. What would I do if these people never let me return to my family? How could I survive without my husband and my little munchkins? How would they survive without me?

Just thinking about it made my heart break. I looked around me for a moment, and saw that no one was paying the least bit of attention to me. They would not care if I indulged in a bit of self-pity.

I usually refrained from crying since I wanted to teach the girls the benefits of self-control. But the girls were not here to see me. I felt very alone and bereft without my family.

I laid my head on the table and began to cry. Well, to be truthful, I blubbered. I sobbed. I wailed. I had more water flowing out of my eyes than Niagara Falls during the rainy season.

I cried myself to sleep.

My next conscious thought after my pity-fest was the sound of voices. My head was still on the table, and it seemed to me that the owners of the voices must have been standing directly behind me.

"She's scared."

"Well, if you were in her place, wouldn't you be scared?"

It was obvious they were talking about me, so I decided to "sleep" a little longer. I made an effort to keep my breathing slow and steady.

"I would. I would suspect that the place was full of crazy people, and that I hadn't a hope for the future."

"I never knew you were such a pessimist!"

"I'm not a pessimist, but from her viewpoint things look pretty bleak."

"Try to assure her that everything will be okay."

There was a long pause. Could that mean that the response was a head nod? I so wish I could see as well as hear. Facial expressions and body language would tell me so much!

"So we are sending her back. How will we keep her from talking?"

I was going home! My heart began to pound so hard I was afraid I would not be able to hear all of the conversation, and I wanted to hear every word.

"We have a rarely used technique that should do the trick."

"This technique, it makes it safe to send her back to her own time?"

"Yes. It's called shielding, and it is perfectly safe if done correctly."

"So you have done this before?"

"Not exactly."

"What do you mean, not exactly?"

"It's not a technique that is commonly used. It can be dangerous. For her."

"What can happen?"

"I will be shielding her memories. It's a tricky business, because if I shield too much, she might forget more than just her trip into our time."

"Like—"

"Like how to brush her teeth, or even how to eat."

"I can see how that could be awkward."

"Or, it might cause damage we cannot predict."

"Damage, what kind of damage?"

"The brain is very complicated, and with all we've studied, there are still some things we don't fully understand. There is always the possibility that something in her brain would cease to function properly."

"Cease to function...you mean she could become a vegetable?"

"I'm afraid so, but only if things go wrong."

"Is it absolutely necessary to mess with her mind?"

"'Mess with her mind' is a rather crude way of putting it, don't you think? I prefer to think of it as a delicate medical procedure."

"But is it necessary?"

"It's necessary if we want to be able to send her back. And you know how important that is."

"What if you make one of those rare mistakes? What if you shield too much and make her into a vegetable?"

"I won't do that."

"How can you be sure? You said you'd never done this before."

"I can be sure because it is too important—our survival depends on it."

"So you believe you can do it right?"

"I have to do it right."

In the tense silence that followed that statement, both men moved away and I could no longer hear their voices. I decided my best course at the moment was to keep my head on the table as if I were still fast asleep. Anyone watching me would assume that I had not overheard a word.

I almost wish I had not. My heart was now pounding so hard I worried it would hammer its way right out of my chest. But this time it was not pounding with excitement, but with fear.

Tears began to silently stream down my cheeks as I thought of all I might lose. I had spent years in school, preparing myself for a career. One slip of the surgeon's tools and I might forget everything I had learned. I might never have the chance to use the education I had spent so many years acquiring.

And then there was my health. I had always had wonderfully good health, but what if that ended? What if the surgeon made a mistake and damaged my eyes, or my ears, or my lungs, or my heart? Would I be able to adapt?

But my true fear was that this process would in some way harm my family. Sure, it would be bad enough if my health was compromised or if I lost the ability to use my education, but my family was everything to me. Anything that affected me, affected my family. I could not stand the thought of my little girls growing up without their mother, or my husband struggling along as a single parent.

My family, my health, my education—my life! One wrong move by the surgeon, one mistake, one slip, and I would cease to be me.

∗ ∗ ∗

I awoke to find my sleeves drenched in tears and the man I had first talked to sitting across the table from me. His kindly I-feel-so-sorry-for-you look disappeared from his face and was replaced with a saccharine sweet, have-I-got-great-news-for-you expression as he saw my open eyes.

"I'm so glad you're awake, I've got great news!"

"Great news?" I asked cautiously as I painfully lifted my head from my arms. My neck and back creaked like an old ship. How many hours had I been sitting in that awkward position?

"Oh yes, very great news. All the forms have been completed, and the decision had been made to send you back to your own time."

"But I thought you guys couldn't send me back because I might talk?" I looked directly into the man's eyes as I asked the question. Whether I ultimately trusted him or not depended on his response, and his body language. How much would he tell me? Would he tell me the whole truth? Was he smooth enough to smile, lie, and chat as if everything was perfect and I was not about to have a procedure done that might adversely affect my life forever?

"I don't think you'll talk," the man said calmly, his smile slipping a bit. "You're smart enough to know that no one would believe you."

"They might."

"Right," the man responded, his smile slipping a bit more, "you think everyone would believe you if you starting talking about a magic door that took you to the future?"

"I wouldn't call it a magic door!"

"What would you call it?"

"A time portal. People have heard of time portals in my time, you know."

"They have?" He looked very confused, and had given up any pretense of the happy-go-lucky, everything-is-peachy-keen persona he had attempted to assume. "People in your time have heard of time portals? How can that be, when they haven't been invented yet?"

"Haven't you ever heard of science fiction?"

"No, what is it?"

"It's when stories are created based on possible scientific advances. Only usually, the scientific advances have bad consequences."

"So you're saying that there has been speculation that time portals are possible?"

"Loads of speculation!"

"And there are supposed to be bad consequences?"

"Loads of bad consequences."

"Tell me more. What kinds of consequences do people speculate might occur? There may be something we haven't thought of. " He pulled out a pad of paper and began to write, forgetting that he was here to convince me that everything was gong to be all right.

I smiled. What a relief to find that humans were basically the same, no matter the time. In the future scientists would continue to use low-tech gadgets like paper and pencil, and they would remain predictably distractible. Mention their field of expertise, tease them with possible unknown theories, and they were hooked. All else was instantly forgotten.

"I would love to talk sci-fi with you, but..."

"But what?"

"Well, didn't you come in here to talk to me for a reason?"

"Talk...oh! I had forgotten. I apologize."

"Apology accepted."

"So, what were we discussing before I got distracted by time travel and its possible unintended consequences?"

"You were telling me that I will be allowed to go home." I watched his face carefully, and was strangely relieved to see the worry reappear. I think he was a sincere man, not smooth at all.

"Right." He pushed his paper and pencil away as if they smelled like bad fish. I had ruined his happy moment.

"You were saying that no one would believe me if I told them about my adventure."

"Right," the man said, nodding his head sadly, "and you said that people would believe. That some people already think time travel is possible."

"I was only saying what I said to see what you would say in case I could get you to say something you didn't really want to say but that was important and worth saying."

"You were saying that you said..." He looked perplexed, as if the sees and says of my sentence had his mental muscles tied up in knots.

"I was conducting an experiment, trying to determine if you could be trusted."

"Oh."

The wounded look on his face helped me make my decision. Here was a man about as smooth as sandpaper, as easily distracted as a five year old, who was upset at the thought that someone might not trust him. He was either an evil genius who was also an exceedingly good actor, or he was a good guy and truly meant me no harm. I decided to go with the good guy theory.

"I couldn't tell anyone about this," I said, wanting to relieve his mind a bit. What kind of guest would I be if I visited in another time and caused problems and stress? "They would think I was nuts!"

"They would?"

"Of course they would!"

"So people don't know anything about time travel? This whole thing, this Science Fiction, it was just something you made up?"

"Oh no, I didn't make up science fiction. The genre is real enough. A lot of people enjoy it because it makes an entertaining story. But very few people believe all that stuff can really happen."

"So you don't want to tell anyone." He said it like a statement, not a question.

"Not likely."

"I knew I could trust you," he said in relief as a smile blossomed on his face.

"So," I said propping my elbows on the table. It was time I got some real answers. "You're sending me back simply because you believe I won't talk? Isn't that rather trusting of you guys?"

"It would be if that were the only reason we were sending you back."

"So tell me, why are you sending me back?"

"The decision was made to return you to your time because we make every effort not to change important events of the past."

That was a shocker! I had expected him to say that I was deemed harmless enough to send home, or they did not want to deprive my children of their mother. But to decide I should be sent home because I was of historical importance, that I had done something…

"Are you saying that I am in some way connected to an important event?"

"You must be, because we found mention of you in our history books. We have no choice but to send you back. You fall within a segment of history that the regulations say must remain unchanged."

Thank goodness for bureaucracy, rules and regulations to the rescue!

I should have just been happy I was being allowed to return to my own time, but I had so many questions. I wanted to know more!

"What do I do to get in the history books?" I asked, unable to hide the excitement from my voice. "Do I do something wonderful and exciting, or boring and minor?" I so hoped that the answer was wonderful and exciting.

"You make a discovery."

"What do I discover?" A discovery sounded so exciting!

"Oh no, I can't tell you that. That would be cheating. But let's just say that the discovery you make does its part to change the world for the better."

"Change the world for the better, hmmm. Well, is it a big change, or a little one?"

"I don't think I should tell you any more."

"Okay, fine, don't tell me any more. But I don't get it. I'm an archaeologist, I study the past. How can I make a discovery that will change the future?"

"Like I said before, I can't tell you, but trust me, it's important."

"When will I make this discovery?"

"Oh, no! I'm certainly not going to give you any clues to that!"

"Well, how am I going to recognize when I've come across this good-enough-for-the-history-books discovery?"

"That's the point. It is better if you don't know anything, so that you won't change the way to do things. If you know any details, you might become so focused on this discovery that you miss another one. And who knows what we will discover is important in the future."

"So you won't tell me when to expect this momentous event?"

"No. Besides, I don't know if you will think it's important or not."

"Okay, fine," I said, as I realized that he truly didn't want to give me the information I wanted. What a spoilsport. "I'll live with the mystery. When do I go back?"

"Just as soon as everything is ready."

"So it isn't as easy as walking back through the door?"

"Of course not!" he said, seemingly surprised that I would have thought such a thing. "If it were, we'd have people wandering in here every day."

I nodded my head to show I understood, and sat silently for about three minutes. When the man did not offer any further explanations I decided to do a little more digging. After all, I might as well put my archaeological training to some good use.

"So, tell me one thing about my history-worthy discovery. Does it have to do with archaeology?"

"That would be telling more than is healthy."

"Okay, tell me this. Would you send me back if I told you I was thinking about going into another field other than archaeology?"

"Yes."

"Ah ha! So it's not an archaeological discovery I make! Or maybe it is, and you think I would make it even if I were in another field."

I looked at the serene expression on the man's face and knew I was digging in the wrong spot. But where should I dig?

"If my discovery didn't have to do with archaeology, what did it have to do with? Was it in another field of science?"

Some of the serenity had left the man's face. I seemed to have made him a little uncomfortable. Was I now digging in the right spot?

"What other field of science have I been interested in? Let's see, I once..."

"The discovery you make does not matter to me right now," the man interrupted tersely. It amazed me to see that all traces of calmness had deserted the poor man. I must have hit a nerve. "The decision has been made to send you back, and that is all I need to tell you."

"So you think. But I think you should tell me what you are holding back. Don't you think I have a right to know?"

"I really cannot tell you much, except, well...I think your children need you."

"Of course my children need me! Don't all children need their parents?"

"Yes, certainly. But the history books are very clear that..."

"What's all this with history books again! No archaeologist has that much room in the history books, not unless they discovered something that totally changes the way people think about the past. Spill the beans, what have I got to do with history books?"

"Well, the history books are clear that it was the influence of both of the parents that allowed your children to do what they did."

"*My children*! Are you saying that *my children* are also in the history books?" It was enough to make a proud mother's heart go pitter-patter. The thought that my little munchkins, the same munchkins who did not yet know how to buy groceries at the store, would grow up to be brilliant, important people—not just important and brilliant to me, which was a given—was fascinating! It was a mother's dream come true.

"Your children will all work together, and it is the fourth one, the one that is not yet born, that is the catalyst of the whole discovery."

"What discovery?" I asked, grabbing the man's arm in my excitement. "What will my children discover?"

"Your children will change the world. Your fourth child will unlock the mystery of how to travel through time. The four of them will then work together to set up the system of time travel we have in place today."

"Time travel?" I yelled, jumping up and pacing around the table. This was big! "My children will discover how to time travel."

"Yes, so you can see why we have to send you back." He smiled at me and pointed to the chair across from him. "Why don't you take a seat while we continue our discussion. I need to explain the procedure. We must proceed very carefully to insure that we don't harm your child."

"My child?"

"Yes, the one that isn't yet born."

"The one—oh my goodness, you said that I would have a fourth child. I'm going to have another child?"

"She will be born in late November of this year."

I counted on my fingers, and reached out with a shaky hand to grab a nearby chair. Sitting suddenly sounded like a fantastic idea.

"I'm pregnant?"

"You are indeed. Congratulations!"

"I'm going to have another girl?"

"Yes, another beautiful, intelligent daughter."

75

I sat for a moment in silence, letting the news soak in. Another child!

"You know, I wasn't expecting this, but the more I think about it, the more excited I get. Tony will be ecstatic, I need to tell him right away."

"I'm afraid you won't be able to do that."

"But I thought you said you were sending me back!"

"We are."

"So what is the problem? Why can't I tell my husband that I'm pregnant?"

"You can't tell him, because you won't remember."

"I won't remember?" I was confused. How could this man be so deluded to think that I could forget all that I had learned here? It was etched into my memory like an inscription on marble.

"You won't remember one minute of your visit here."

It hit me like a ton of bricks—the conversation I had overheard while my captors thought I was sleeping.

"What are you going to do to me?" I asked, fear creeping into my voice.

"I'm sorry to say, but we are going to mess with your mind."

Chapter 8

MY FIRST WAKING THOUGHT WAS that I really needed to buy a new pillow. This one was as hard as a rock.

I lifted my head and opened my eyes, trying to focus on my surroundings. For some reason, my eyes refused to cooperate. Everything around me was one big, messy blur.

I tried to compel my eyes to zoom in on my pillow, thinking that it was a big enough target that my eyes could succeed with ease. It would give them confidence, make them feel good about themselves.

But they refused to cooperate, categorically denying my right to boss them around. They did deem it acceptable to give me an image though, one of a big, flat surface with no definition, and definitely no pillow-ness.

I was not pleased. I wanted to see my pillow.

I reached down to grab said pillow and found only air. I reached lower and found the cold hard surface of a table.

At that point my eyes finally took pity on me and began to work properly. As my surroundings came into focus I realized what an idiot I was. I was not in my bed at all, but in the lab. I must have fallen asleep while working on a project.

"Ouch, that hurts," I muttered as my movements made a crick in my neck evident.

"Well, that answers the age-old question of why we lay on big, fluffy beds to sleep, instead of propping ourselves against a table to catch a few winks," I grumbled. "My usual preference for a comfy bed is best after all."

"Oooooh," I groaned as another small movement created an avalanche of pain. I was stiff and achy all over—but most of the tenderness I felt was centered on my neck. I must have slept with my head turned in an awkward position, since that usually trouble-free connector between my head and body now felt like it belonged to a robot that had been left out to rust. For decades.

"I'd better change that to centuries," I grumbled, as every slight movement exponentially increased the pain in my neck. "Too bad I'm not a robot. I'm sure a robot could have a pain-in-the-neck-optomy, while we poor humans just get to suffer. Lucky robots."

As I stretched my arms over my head to find the status of other potentially painful parts of my body, I wondered how I had ever fallen asleep in that uncomfortable position. It was not normal for me. When it came to the old Shakespearean question "To doze, or not to doze," I had always chose the latter. Unless I was safe and sound in my own home.

The last thing I recalled—my last memory before I took an unplanned vacation to the land slumber—was turning off the lights so that I could better view the fluorescent specimens.

Which were still sitting, right where I left them, waiting for me to finish up and head home. A glance at my watch relieved my mind a bit, since it seemed I could not have been asleep for more than thirty minutes. If I buckled down now, I should be able to complete my work and get home before that frail glowing orb in the sky was replaced by its dazzling bright sibling.

As I worked, a miniscule voice in the back of my mind whispered little annoying messages about something I had forgotten—something that I should not forget. Something important.

"If it's really important, I'll remember it," I muttered with a sigh. "People always do, if it's truly important."

"Why, there's even an old saying about important things always being remembered, if they are truly important."

"So I might as well stop worrying about it, and let it come to me when it wants to."

I blocked those annoying whispers as best I could and focused. About an hour later I rubbed my eyes, wrote down the last calculation, and gave a deep sigh. Finally the project was complete, and I could relax for a day or two before I needed to work on the next assignment.

"I'm going to go home, snuggle into my bed, and sleep all day. Or at least, I'll sleep until almost time for my first class. I'm not about to pay all this money for a college education to sleep through it. I'm going to absorb every scrap of knowledge I can."

I packed up my possessions and headed for home.

I was fine until I pulled into a parking space in university housing. I had no trouble driving home, no problems finding a place to park—even the traffic lights were all with me. But as soon as I turned the car key to the off position, BAM! It seemed as if the key turned the car off as it turned the annoying voice in my head on. One minute the radio was playing music, the next I was engulfed in the feeling that something important was still forgotten. And when I say engulfed, I mean engulfed. Gone was the little whispering voice; it had been replaced by loud, obnoxious, overwhelming screams.

I sat quietly in the car for a moment trying to figure out what I could have forgotten that was so important. I looked in my backpack, and yes, I had both my completed project and the key to the lab. I replayed the steps I took to leave Denny Hall and specifically recalled locking both the lab and the outside doors.

I was sitting in my car, so I knew I had my car keys.

What could I have forgotten?

With a shrug, I decided that whatever it was, it was not worth the loss of sleep. I exited the car and headed for the one place where I could put my cares aside, recharge my mental batteries, and rest undisturbed.

I sighed as I remembered that the lock in the front door usually stuck a bit, and that I would need to waste several precious moments— moments better spent sleeping—fighting the door for my right to enter. As I wielded the key in preparation for battle, I heard a click, the knob turned, and the door was flung open.

"I looked first, I promise," declared a beaming little girl of about eight, with long brown hair, big dark eyes, and a dimple in one cheek. "I heard your footsteps and I looked out the window. I'm hungry!"

I stood in the doorway looking at the little girl with the big eyes. Who was she? Why was she in my house? Should I know her?

"Daddy said he wants to sleep ten more minutes, so I should play with my sisters. But I'm hungry!" the girl whispered, and the smile on her face was quickly replaced with a pleading look. "Can you make me some cheese toast? Please?"

Again the same three questions flew around my head: Who was she, should I know her, and why was she in my house?

"Please, please, please," the little girl continued to beg when I failed to respond.

I stood immobile, so tired I was unable to think properly.

The child—obviously the decisive type— took charge of the situation. She grabbed my hand, pulled me inside, closed the front door, checked to see that it was locked, and then pulled me into the kitchen.

As I stepped into the kitchen what had been mild confusion turned to intense shock. My world was suddenly off kilter, spinning madly out of control, headed on a collision course with something big, bad, and horrible. Because in the kitchen, as at home as at home can be, were two additional little girls.

Now I had nine questions zipping around my head. The same three as before: Who was she, should I know her, and why was she in my house—only times three.

Two of the three girls, one of which was the girl from the door, looked so much alike they could easily be mistaken for twins. But an observant person—which I was—would notice the difference of two inches, and realize that the two could not be twins since the second child was probably only about six years old while the first was around eight.

Right as that thought passed through my mind the second girl saw me and bestowed a smile on me that brightened the entire room. Before I had a chance to wonder at her reaction to my entrance, she tossed down the crayon in her hand, jumped up off the floor, and wrapped her little arms around my waist. After a thorough hug she picked up her coloring book and crayons and transferred them to the table.

"Toast please," she requested with more of that smile that could melt the coldest heart.

"Morning," yelled the third child in the room, a cherub of about three years with big brown eyes and a head full of riotous golden curls. She scrambled up from the floor where she had been playing with toy cars and gave a tremendous squeeze to my leg.

"Cheese toast, cheese toast, cheese toast," the cherub chanted into my leg.

"Do you all want cheese toast?" I questioned the three obviously hungry children.

"Yes please," they chorused.

I smiled. I could not help myself. I had no clue who these three adorable children were or why they had been deposited in my house, but I certainly was not going to let them go hungry. They were entirely too cute and sweet.

I would ask a few questions as soon as I had gotten some food into them. Children were usually more compliant when they had full stomachs. They were sure to give me the whole story on their presence here after I had fed them.

As I prepared the cheese toast, I watched the little girls out of the corner of my eye. These girls got along so well together, and they really looked very much alike. It was obvious they were related, most likely they were sisters.

Then, remembering the oldest girl saying her dad had told her to play with her sisters, I knew my supposition was correct.

I finished the three pieces of toast, placed a piece of cheese on each, and put them in the oven to broil. When the cheese started to bubble and brown on top I took the cheese toast out of the oven and I was placing a piece of toast on each of three plates when the rest of what the oldest girl had said popped into my head.

"Just where is their daddy?" I whispered to myself.

Right on cue I heard a loud thump upstairs, and then footsteps running down the stairs. I pasted a smile on my face in preparation for the next surprise I knew must be coming.

I was not quite prepared for the full-grown male who sprinted into the kitchen and halted just inside the doorway. For no good reason my heart fluttered at the sight of him, though he did not look in the least antagonistic. He looked—he looked—well, he looked exactly like the father of these three little girls should look. The same big dark eyes, the same olive complexion, the same dark hair as the two older girls.

He took one look at me and sighed in relief. Not the reaction I expected.

"I smelled toast, and I was afraid Becca had decided to try her hand at cooking. I was afraid I would not make it down the stairs before the house caught fire," the man explained with a sheepish grin.

"Daddy," the oldest girl said in offended tones. "I know not to cook without you or Mama here. I waited for Mama. She made the toast."

I smiled, and then gulped. Now I knew that little thing that had been bugging me that I had forgotten. And even though I still could not remember the details, I somehow knew that this man was my husband, and these sweet, adorable little girls were my daughters.

Chapter 9

I TOOK A FIVE-HOUR NAP hoping that the wonderful healing powers of slumber would restore my memory. But I awoke in the same state I had gone to sleep, completely lacking the ability to remember the people who probably meant the most in my life.

But sleep had not been a useless endeavor since I now felt able to handle whatever was thrown my way—as long as it was not thrown too fast or too hard.

As I helped bundle the girls into the car I realized that I was one lucky amnesiac. I might not be able to remember this lovely family, but at least they were a lovely family.

Imagine the horror a person would feel if she lost her memory and was presented with a passel of brats, and told that she was responsible for those brats. Not only responsible for taking care of them, but responsible for creating them.

The worst would be not to know what you had done wrong, that data would be unavailable. You would not be able to go back over your parenting style and refine it. You would not know if you had been too strict or too lenient, too distant or too smothering.

Why, a person in that situation would have to do an archaeological-type dig on her own life! Only instead of digging through dirt, she would dig through morals, practices, beliefs…

My thoughts got no further, because as I placed the three year old into her car seat, the child gave such a beautiful smile it instantly melted my heart. She looked like such an angel, the blonde curls making a halo. So I decided to reign in my wandering thoughts and get my mind back on the job, which was to learn everything I could about this family so that I could regain my memories of them.

Of course, I had already discovered that even though these girls were nice and sweet, they fell far short of being the perfect angels they looked.

Oddly enough, it gave me more comfort than worry. My guess was that deep down in the depths of my soul was the belief that children should be allowed to be children, complete with occasions of temper, tears, and selfishness.

In my Anthropology classes I was always amazed not so much at the differences in cultures, but in the similarities. How fascinating it was that every culture I had ever studied had some sort of marriage and family group, a belief in a higher power, and fermented beverages.

I found it amusing that every human on the planet had a deep-seated desire to take their family to church and then go out for a beer!

Every culture also had crime, jealousy, and meanness. And although I certainly did not want to promote those tendencies, I accepted that they were a part of what makes us human.

I felt that my job as a parent was not to eradicate those oh-so-human negative tendencies, but to teach my children how to recognize them, understand them, and keep them in check.

How could this be accomplished if the children were perfect little robots that never slipped?

Besides, as slips go, the one I recently witnessed was rather minor.

I had been awakened at one point in my nap by the high-pitched sound of children arguing. One minute I was sound asleep, enjoying the relaxation of quiet dreams, the next I was dumped into a waking nightmare of toddler screeches and little girl shrieks. My impression was that it must have become very heated, very fast.

At first I was horrified, until I really listened to the words being shouted. I could not help but smile when I realized the crux of the argument.

This cacophony of noise was due to a disagreement brought on by a game of pretend. All three girls wanted to assume the star part of Princess Jasmine, but no one wanted to be stuck with the part of a yucky boy. But there were only so many good girl parts, and besides, what good was a princess without a prince? (I'm not sure if the girls realized that technically Aladdin was not a prince, but it was clear they knew he was a boy.)

Even though there had been yelling, there was no hitting. I was impressed that the girls had immediately quieted when they were reminded that their mom had worked in the lab all night and was now trying to sleep. And they followed their dad's suggestion that they play Snow White instead. In addition to the all-important princess part, the queen was a nice juicy female role, and all seven dwarfs could be played by one person, which compensated for the fact that they were male.

Now I had rested, the girls had played, and my husband had studied. It was time to leave the safety of our home and venture out into the big, scary world of toys.

Yes, it was time to visit that much dreaded, feared-by-parents-everywhere world of unlimited temptations, otherwise known as the toy store. At least, that was how I felt parents should view a visit to the toy store.

I did not want to subject myself to such torture, but what other option did I have? The entire family was scheduled to visit my sister-in-law's house the next day to participate in a birthday party for a little nephew turning five.

Honestly, how could we show up at the birthday party without a present—an appropriate present, which could only be purchased in the temptation-laden-torture-chamber of the toy store? The birthday boy would be devastated, his parents scandalized, and these sweet little girls humiliated.

I knew my duty as a parent. I would throw back my shoulders, take a deep breath, and enter the battlefield where the acquisition of toys was the prize, and tears the ammunition.

Internally, another battle raged. I knew I had parenting responsibilities, but how was I going to get my school work done if I was supposed to spend several hours shopping for a gift today, and then spend several more at a child's birthday party tomorrow?

One side of me applauded parents like my husband and myself who put family first, pushing aside other obligations.

The other side felt that this family had their priorities mixed up if they felt that a child's party was more important than a university degree.

I could not decide which part was correct, so the internal battle raged on as we continued our journey to the toy store.

91

The ride in the car was uneventful as we approached the battleground. What kinds of tortures were being planned? Three little girls, running around a toy store, begging for toys that I was sure we could not afford. Should I expect wheedling, crying—possibly a temper tantrum?

I took a deep breath to calm my racing heart. Possibly, just possibly, the terror I anticipated would not be as bad as I imagined. I would have to wait and see exactly how bad the girls would behave.

As we pulled into the parking lot, I turned to study the cherubs in the back seat. Yes, they certainly looked cherub-like, with their faces glowing with expected joy. Each girl had the most beautiful smile lighting up her face as she anticipated the treasures waiting for her within the building.

Sadly, I shook my head. It would be near impossible to control the natural greed of these three girls. I would have felt sorry for myself—this was going to be a horrible experience—but I had to reserve my energy for more important things, like tantrums, or tears.

The girls contained their exuberance as we crossed the parking lot to the door. I braced myself for the worst as we entered into the paradise of all children, the toy store. As I felt my body tense for battle, I glanced at the man by my side to assure myself that he was ready for what was about to ensue. I was shocked to see that he was totally at ease, with a pleasant smile on his face.

Had he never taken children to a toy store? Did he not have a clue what tortures were in store for us? Why was he not bracing himself for the ordeal to come?

"Mommy, look! I want that, Mommy, I want that!" the three-year-old cherub yelled in excitement. "Daddy, look! Look Daddy!"

So it began, just as I had foreseen. The little angels would now be transformed into little devils. The floodgates of greed were open and there would be no stopping the deluge.

I looked at the child's father. Did he understand the import of the child's words? Was he ready to battle the innate greed of these children?

To my surprise, he still appeared composed and unworried. He calmly reached down and picked up the budding shopaholic, and gently turned her face until the two made eye contact.

"Do you remember why we came to the store today?" His voice was serene and unruffled. I could detect no disquiet in his stance or voice that might lead me to believe he was unsure of his success in this skirmish.

"Yes, Daddy. We buy toy," the cherub chirped excitedly, as the magnetic pull of the desired toy forced her gaze and her finger toward the coveted prize. "We buy that toy!"

"You think your cousin will like that toy?" The man must be either a saint or a superhero, to be able to keep his fear in check so well. My heart was galloping so fast it could win the Kentucky Derby three times in a row and still keep going.

"No, I want it. Buy me toy!"

"Zoe, look at me. I need to tell you something." I heard the calmness in his voice, and I was amazed after that outburst—and very nervous. Was this the beginning of a much dreaded temper tantrum?

The little one's gaze remained glued to the desired toy. Undaunted, Tony gently turned the child's face until she was again facing him.

"I asked if your cousin would like the toy because it is his birthday tomorrow, remember?"

"Yes, we go to party!"

"Right. And now we are at the store to get a present for your cousin...only for your cousin," he said firmly.

"But I like it. I want it," came the reply, with tears of greed beginning to glint in her eyes.

"Of course you want it," calmly replied the man with the wallet, "but we are not shopping for toys for you today. We'll do that another day. Now we are looking for a present for your cousin."

The little cherub's bottom lip started to tremble, and wails of temper appeared to be imminent.

"I read you a story at bedtime last night. Do you remember what it was about?"

"Yes," came the wobbly reply, "bears."

"Right, and do you remember what the bears were doing?"

"Uh-huh. They got the gimmies! I 'member."

"Good. Now, do you remember our rule about shopping? We take turns getting toys. And if you get the gimmies like the bears did, I won't be able to buy you any toys next time we go shopping for toys."

"Why, Daddy?"

"Because taking turns is our rule. And today is not your turn, it is your cousin's."

"But I want it," whispered the sad child.

"I know you do sweetie-kins," I said, trying to be helpful.

She turned her huge, sad, tear-filled eyes my way. How could I deny anything to such a face? But if I gave in now, I knew it would mean years of more tears, and probably tantrums.

And then inspiration hit!

"Look, Zoe," I said, injecting my voice with a modicum of excitement. "I've got a notebook here, and I can write down this toy to start your Christmas list!"

"Christmas list?" Her eyes suddenly looked a bit less teary, and her head tilted to the side as she thought about the joys of Christmas gifts. The other two girls suddenly moved closer to listen.

"Yes, as we look around today, tell me what you want to add to your Christmas list. I'll make a separate page for each of you. Then everyone will know what you want."

"But Christmas is forever from now," Becca chimed in, ever the helpful older sister.

"It seems that way now, but it will be here before you know it."

"Please Mommy, Daddy, can we get one toy today?" Maddie asked, smiling timidly.

That timid smile almost proved more powerful than any weapon invented by man. It was sweet, genuine, and almost irresistible.

The war would have been lost right there if I had not looked at Tony and immediately recognized that he was ready to give in. A father could remain strong against tantrums, but sweetness, well sweetness got you in the heart.

"Oh, but that would spoil the fun!" I jumped in, to keep my husband from caving and making our lives miserable for years to come. "If we bought you what you wanted right now, no one else could have fun giving you presents. Wouldn't that be sad for them?"

Two serious nods and one watery smile showed me that parental logic had prevailed—for now, at least.

I was very confused. I accepted that this was my family, but I could not remember my life with them. I had no history to fall back on, no experiences to learn from. Yet, when push came to shove, I'd known exactly what to say.

Did that mean I had it? Did I have that marvelous force of legends, the amazing shrewdness in myths, the wonderful tenacity from tall tales? In other words, was maternal instinct alive and well, working away unseen within *my* brain?

If so, would it help me through other trials?

Enough thinking about the mysteries of the human brain—and lost memories. There was shopping to be done, and lists to be created.

Luckily, once the gimmie hurdle was overcome, the rest of the shopping session was uneventful. An appropriate gift for the young boy cousin was chosen, huge wish lists were created, and everyone in the family, including the girls, left the toy store satisfied by the experience.

The only odd event occurred as my toy-satiated family headed back to the comforts of home.

We drove down the road, and I contemplated how amazingly pleasant this family outing to the toy store had been, especially since none of the three children in the car had acquired a single toy. Most amazing of all was that the children were not scarred by their parent's refusal to provide them with the smallest of treasures; instead they were chatting and laughing happily in the backseat.

"Daddy," called little Maddie, "why are those people dressed so funny?"

"What people, sweetie?" Tony asked. We had just stopped at a red light, and there were quite a few people walking down the sidewalks. "Who is dressed funny?"

"Those people, there," Maddie said, pointing to a bus stop. "They are wearing funny hats, and they don't have coats on. They must be cold. Don't you think they are funny looking?"

I looked at the bus stop where the child was pointing, and sure enough there was a man and a woman waiting for a bus.

The man was dressed in a tuxedo the style of which I had often seen in movies from the 1920s. Fortunately for him, this meant that he had long sleeves.

The woman was wearing a long flowing dress of a shiny material, with no sleeves whatsoever. Her only protection from the cold and wet of the Pacific Northwest weather was a skimpy feather boa loosely wrapped around her shoulders, which was very poor protection indeed. Both were wearing hats, but not the rainproof or warm hats I would expect at this time of year.

Instead, both the man and the woman had stayed true to what I assumed were their costumes; the woman's hat sported a feather, while the man was wearing a top hat.

Could there be a play being put on in the area? Was the couple on their way to a dress rehearsal?

But why should they be in costume already? It made no sense for them to get dressed at home and chance spills and splashes on public transportation. It was my understanding that costumes were expensive, so actors and actresses put them on at the theater.

Oddly enough the pair had chosen to wait out in open for the bus, disregarding the little shelter provided by the bus stop. So they were in costume, standing in the rain when shelter was available, not wearing the proper attire for the weather.

As I gazed at the couple, I was surprised to notice that they appeared to be unaffected by the cold, and impervious to stares. Nor did they seem to be part of some publicity stunt, trying to attract attention.

As we waited for the light to change to green, a car pulled up to the bus stop and the couple moved over to get inside. That solved the mystery of why they were at the curb rather than the shelter.

I watched them move the few feet to the car, and I noticed the strange manner in which they held themselves. Their backs looked inflexible, as if instead of a many-boned spine, their backbone had been fused into a solid pole.

How odd, I thought. These people walked with ramrod-straight backs. They were going to have to overcome that particular posture if they planned to act in a play or movie. Most books I'd read made note of the epidemic of slouching common to the era; no one in the roaring 20s sported a ramrod-straight posture.

Come to think of if, no one I have ever heard of had such a posture.

A fleeting memory, just out of reach, flashed into my consciousness and left swiftly. Somewhere I had seen someone with this posture. Now, just where had it been?

Chapter 10

AS THE LIGHT OF MORNING sun hit my eyelids, I decided it must be time to leave the land of slumber and start a new day.

If I could convince my eyes to open, that was. They really did not like that transition period when they were forced to leave the relaxing darkness of night to be assaulted by that bright orb which sometimes showed itself in the morning sky.

My eyes told me that they found the entire process extremely unfair!

I convinced them to open a slit, and both my eyes and I (or should I say the three of us?) were pleased to discover that there was no pain waiting to sneak in with the sun's rays.

A little at a time I persuaded my eyes to widen, until they were finally fully open and ready for a new day. Now all I had to do was roll over, sit up, and get out of bed.

But my movements were arrested as my eyes focused on the man sleeping beside me.

As if someone had started playing twenty different movies in my head at the same time, memories flooded my brain, engulfing me with a kaleidoscope of images made up of the wonderful times I'd shared with this man. Interspersed among the picnics, movies, berry picking, and long walks were discussions about everything under the sun. Discussions I had enjoyed very much.

My heart swelled with love as the realization hit me that I truly enjoyed being with this man who was my husband. It swelled even more as I thought about how amazing it was that I could talk to him about absolutely everything.

Tears poured down my cheeks as my heart overfilled with emotion. This man was not simply my husband—he was my best friend!

I was such a sap, to cry like this. A grown woman should not blubber like a baby simply because she realized she loved her husband!

I wiped the tears from my face and took a deep breath. I would not cry. There was no reason to cry. I was a happy woman, with a lovely family, a wonderful husband—

I burst into sobs again, but this time the tears had nothing to do with joy, but with fear. I had a real, legitimate reason to cry.

My heart, recently overfilled with joyous emotion, now felt hollow. Terror gripped me in a stranglehold as I realize how close I had been to losing the people I held dearest.

What in the world had happened to me yesterday? What horrific event had occurred to make me forget the most important people in my life? There were no humans on this earth who were more valuable to me than my family. I could not imagine anything that could make me forget them for even an instant, much less an entire day!

I sniffed back my tears and reached around to the back of my head, feeling for the lump that must exist somewhere on my cranial region. Nothing felt swollen or tender. The bump must be there!

There was only one explanation for my memory loss—I must have slipped and fallen at the lab. If I felt long enough, I'd find a nice fat lump that justified forgetting my family for an entire day.

"People didn't forget their nearest and dearest for no reason. The bump must be here somewhere," I whispered as I frantically searched my head. Sadly, I could find no lumps, no sore spots.

My hands stopped their frenzied search for bumps and bruises as a worse thought leapt to the fore. I had heard of students succumbing to the stress of school and family who had lost their sanity. If I had not fallen and knocked myself unconscious, I must fall into the too-weak-to-handle-the-stress category. That would account for the true craziness that occurred when I forgot my sweet, wonderful husband, and my oh-so-precious little girls.

"Maybe I should offer myself as a test subject for the psychology department," I mused under my breath. "If I'm studied, it might help other people who suffer similar type memory losses."

I could not get over the horror of forgetting not only the man I had promised to devote my life to, but also my darling children! How could I? Without my family, I'd be...I'd be...well frankly, I'd be nothing.

A flush of heat enveloped me and droplets of sweat materialized on my upper lip. Yesterday was a close call. I could barely believe I had succeeded in masking my memory loss—it had been a horrendous struggle.

"But now, thank goodness, everything is back to normal," I whispered, looking at my husband to make sure my mutterings had not disturbed his slumber. "I remember my munchkins, my hubby, and the reason all those silly jokes are funny. They sure weren't funny yesterday!"

I successfully climbed out of bed without waking Tony and made my way downstairs. I wanted time to think, and the early morning minutes before the girls awoke would be the only minutes available. It was essential that I made the most of them.

"There's something odd about the way I lost my memory and got it back. I'll have to do a little research before I talk to the psychology department—see if maybe it's somehow normal."

I stopped in front of the mirror in the living room and took a good look at my face. I looked normal enough. "Yet," I said with a shrug, "I do have a tendency to talk to myself, which is supposed to be a sign of an unstable mind."

"Talking to myself aside, maybe I should concentrate on my two mysteries, because really, it does seem like two. The first is why did I lose my memory, and the second is what made my memory come back."

"I should probably focus on my time in the lab. My memory loss began when I woke up in the lab. So what do I remember before that?"

I moved into the kitchen and flipped on the espresso maker. This required coffee. "The last thing I remember was placing my hand on the knob of door to leave the lab."

"But that doesn't make any sense!" I said worriedly as I got a cup out of the cabinet. "I woke up at the table. How did I get from the door to the table?"

"I've simply got to remember!" I declared, slamming my fist down on the counter in frustration. "I will not let my mind fail, I won't let myself go crazy, I will remember!

I scooped coffee into the receptacle and tamped it down. When the light signaled that the machine was ready, I flipped the switch and watched the foamy coffee stream into my cup.

The aroma alone was enough to wake me up. I breathed in deeply, thoroughly enjoying the robust richness.

Hazy images of a city drifted into my mind, strange, fuzzy images so unclear that I was unable to make out any details—almost as if I was viewing the city through gossamer curtains. I was not even sure why I thought it was a city. Its city-likeness seemed to come from the solid, stable shapes I took to be buildings, which were unfortunately confused by an abundance of light that danced about in beautiful, fluid, iridescent patterns—unfortunate because the light patterns hid any details. If only I could pull back those curtains, I felt a glimpse of the city would help me solve the mystery of my memory mush mind.

I sat down at the table and took a sip of coffee. It was absolutely perfect—rich, hot, robust, and fragrant—just as coffee should be. As I closed my eyes to enjoy another sip, I playfully imagined the curtains of my mind being pulled aside.

The next second I had quickly, but shakily, placed the cup of hot coffee on the table. My trembling fingers could not be trusted to guide the coffee to my mouth—they were much more likely to spill the entire cup down the front of my nightgown.

It was not the fault of my poor fingers; I placed the blame firmly with my brain. That organ was responsible for sending messages to my fingers, but was too distracted. Under the circumstances, I could not rely on my brain to focus long enough to relay the proper orders to my poor fingers.

In reality, I could not truly blame my brain for being so distracted. The curtain had disappeared. My amazed brain was inundated with images of a strange city, a city I knew I had never seen before.

Or had I? The vividness was amazing—so amazing, in fact, that I was sure that this city could not have been dreamed, but must be real! I did not believe that humans were capable of dreaming with this much detail, this much color, and this much imagination.

But if this city was a memory, when had I seen it? The city was so different from any other I had ever encountered.

I closed my eyes, determined to recapture as many details as possible of this wondrous city. There must be something about it I needed to remember, needed to notice, needed to understand. Otherwise, why had it become so clear and vivid? What message was I supposed to recognize?

I jumped up from the table and ran into the living room to grab a piece of paper and a pencil. I could only figure out one reason to have this vision of this city. It must have something to do with my memory loss. To understand the glitch in my memory, I needed to explore the city in my memory.

First impressions were always a great place to start, so I mentally reclosed the gossamer curtains, waited a moment, and then pulled them open again. My first impression was that I was viewing a beautiful garden.

Every building, as far as the eye could see, was draped in garments of greenery. Glass windows sparkled merrily, reflecting both the brilliance of the sun and a wealth of flowers of every color. Vines grew thickly on buildings, allowing only flashes of stone to peek through. No blacktop or concrete was visible in the streets, only trees and lush grass. Even the rooftops were not neglected—they were planted with gardens of every style and design.

What a concept! The passengers of a plane flying overhead would be hard pressed to differentiate any part of the city from the surrounding countryside. All they would see were green hills and valleys covered by lush vegetation.

First impression noted. The city was a giant garden. What else? Were there any people?

I focused harder but had no luck. The city I could see fine, but the residents remained unclear. There were just a bunch of blurry dots scuttling around on a carpet of green. I decided to once again try the trick of closing the gossamer curtains and reopening them.

As the curtains moved aside, I was staggered by the vision before me. My first view of the city had been from afar, perfect for viewing the overall effect of a garden city. But closing and opening the curtains had caused me to zoom in much closer, so close I could make out individual faces and styles of clothing.

It was the styles of clothing that confused me. The way members of a society dressed told volumes about the values of the culture. Whether it was color choices, types of fabrics, or even the amount of clothing, members of a culture defined themselves as a part of that culture by their dress.

But here there was no cohesion, no definition of culture. It was as if I were viewing a gigantic movie studio, with hundreds of epic movies being shot at the same time.

I recognized the clothing of civilizations from many different eras and geographic locations amongst the population of the garden city. I saw Roman gladiators walking together with seventeenth century courtiers, who strolled alongside 1920s flappers, who conversed with WWII fighter pilots, who were lunching with Viking warriors, who sat next to Samurai warriors, who chatted with girls in poodle skirts…well, the mix of cultures and times just went on and on.

As I gazed at the vision before me, I realized that odd clothing aside, all the residents of the city shared a common element. All held themselves stiffly, as if the individual vertebrae of their spinal column had been fused into one solid backbone.

109

It looked somehow familiar.

Then I remembered the man and woman that Maddie had noticed at the bus stop.

Relief flooded my body as I theorized that those two characters at the bus stop must have temporarily shorted out my brain. This strange but beautiful city, vivid though it may be, was simply a weirdo inspired crazy dream.

Which raised the question: Did the dream of the city somehow cause my memory loss?

I was certain that was not possible. I had lost my memory well before I saw those two characters. Instead of bringing about my loss of memory, they must be responsible for restoring it.

Still, the most critical mystery remained unsolved: Why had I lost my memory in the first place?

Chapter 11

"I AM SO SICK OF this project," I muttered for the sixth time in one hour.

"Stop grumbling," my classmate Erica scolded. "All that whining isn't going to get your work done any faster."

I glared at her grumpily. What right had she to criticize my complaining? She had finished the project fifteen minutes ago, and had even already rechecked her work.

"Cheer up," Erica said as she looked over my shoulder, "all you have left to do is the last segment. It'll be a breeze."

"A breeze!" I exclaimed. "It looked to me like the last segment was the most time consuming for you."

"That's right, you'll be done in a snap," Erica said absentmindedly as she gathered up a stack of papers and frantically thrust them into her backpack.

I did not like that half of the papers she had shoved into her backpack were mine—even if they were ones I had decided were too messy to turn in so I had made clean copies. Erica did not know that I had made copies, so as far as she knew she was taking papers that would set my work back days—very uncharacteristic of my ultra-considerate, always thoughtful friend.

Also out of character was the way Erica had so quickly changed from cheerful-to-a-tee to distracted-beyond-belief. If I did not know better, I would think that Erica was hiding something from me.

I put down my pencil and looked closely at her face. My heart sank as I realized that Erica's gaze was glued to the papers in her hands. She was doing everything in her power to avoid meeting my eyes.

As a mother of three, I recognized the classic if-I-don't-look-at-you-you-can't-ask-me-questions stance. It was crystal clear that Erica had something to hide.

It was obvious I had a job to do. I must not let Erica leave the lab until I found out if what she was hiding was personal, and therefore none of my business, or project related and likely to make my life miserable.

"Erica."

"Hmmmm?"

A causal observer would assume that Erica was extremely busy—that the papers she diligently shuffled were of extreme importance. But I was not the causal observer. I knew that mixed in with Erica's once pristine project papers were my rejected papers and various discarded notes. Methodical Erica had created a jumbled mess.

"Erica, look me in the eye and tell me that this last part of the project will be quick."

Erica stole a quick look in my direction before she grabbed the papers I was working on and began to industriously stuff them into her backpack.

"I'll keep those if you don't mind," I said as I calmly retrieved my papers. "Come on, tell me. How long did it take you to finish?"

Erica's face flushed as she realized she had snatched my work right from under my hands. She turned away from me for a second, probably to regain her composure, and then faced me with a fake smile that I knew from past experience meant she had bad news to impart that she would try to play off as good.

"Not to worry," she said with a forced smile, "it only took me three or four hours. And I'm a bit of a perfectionist."

"You're a perfectionist." I looked at Erica's body language, noting her inability to hide her discomfort. Her uptightness changed to confusion as I continued sarcastically, "Right, thanks for the compliment, Erica."

I hated to do it to the girl, but work or no work, this was too good an opportunity to pass up. Erica had a gullible streak that she had never been able to tame. I had a teasing streak I had no desire to tame. We made quite a good team.

I lowered my eyes to the table in an attempt to look like a hound dog that had been offered a juicy steak but given a dry twig.

"I didn't know you thought my work was so sloppy," I said with a big sigh. "I had no idea you viewed my efforts as slapdash, shoddy, and inferior. I always thought…"

"No, that's not what I meant! It's just that I have a really bad tendency to triple and quadruple check all my results."

"Is that supposed to make me feel better, that you don't think I'm sloppy, just careless?" I hung my head even lower to show the dept of my despondency.

"No, no, no!" Erica exclaimed. "I didn't mean that at all. It's just that you are so much better at the measurements and drawings than I am. You can trust your work. I make so many mistakes that I always have to go back over my measurements again and again."

I lifted my head until I could focus the rays of hope beaming from my eyes upon my uncomfortable friend. "Are you sure that is what you meant? Because I know I am at a slight disadvantage time-wise because of my kids. I want you to tell me if it is affecting my work."

"No, trust me, it is not affecting your work," Erica said in her sincerest voice. "I've noticed from our first class together how you focus much better than most of us, I think because you have to. You don't have time to redo the same project over and over, so you do it right the first time."

"Are you sure?" I pleaded as pitifully as I was able. "I mean, I'm working so hard to make sure my family doesn't lose out because of school, but I also want to be sure that my school work doesn't lose out because I don't have any extra time. It's such a juggling act!"

I put my hand to my forehead and sighed dramatically. Cautiously I peeked at Erica to see how she was taking it.

I must have overplayed that last part a bit, because Erica was sitting back on her stool with her arms crossed in front of her chest.

"Very funny," she said.

"Erica, I'm proud of you," I exclaimed with a grin. "You were much quicker this time figuring out that I was kidding."

"Well, the joke's on you now," Erica said as she raised one eyebrow, "because you have several hours of work left to do…and I'm done."

"Sad—but true." This time the sigh was real.

"What is really sad," said Erica in disgust as she looked into her backpack, "is this mess! Whatever was I thinking?"

"You were thinking that you wanted to get out of here before I could ask you too many questions about the project."

"But look at this mess!"

"It's not that bad. It will only take a few minutes to straighten out. And if it makes you feel any better, those papers of mine mixed in with yours, you can throw them away. I have copies."

"What do you mean—papers of yours?"

"Just look."

Erica pulled an unruly stack of papers out and began to sort. She shook her head and grimaced as the pile of papers labeled with the initials VT got taller and taller.

"I must be a kleptomaniac and not even know it. It would have been a disaster if you hadn't already copied all this work."

"If I hadn't already copied it, you wouldn't have been able to get away with it. I am quite able to protect my property from petty thieves."

"Petty thief. Good one. Thanks."

"Thought you would like it. No problem."

Erica finished packing her backpack but made no move toward the door, which was fine with me since one thing she had said earlier still bothered me.

"Erica," I said casually.

Maybe too casually, because Erica's "Yes?" was very suspicious.

"I know you are finished and probably want to get out of here, but...well, I have to ask.

What did you mean about how you don't trust your work? You do fantastic work!"

"It might turn out okay, but I have to struggle to get it right—your work is better."

"What *are* you talking about?"

"What am I talking about? Remember that project that we had to turn in two weeks ago? The one the professor gave back to us yesterday. What grade did you make on it?"

"Let's see," I muttered as I thought. "I had a lot of trouble with that project because I almost ran out of time. I had to take Becca to a doctor's appointment and Zoe had an earache."

"So, what did you make?"

"I made a 3.9.

"A 3.9 is about a 98 percent, right?"

"Right."

"So, why didn't you make a 100 percent? What was wrong with it?"

"What was wrong with it was a stupid little mistake in the appendix."

"What kind of stupid little mistake?"

"I should have put one of the measurements in two different places, but I only put it in one. I got dinged for it."

"Right, and I made 3.4, and I didn't make one mistake, I made many mistakes and they weren't quite so teeny."

"Erica, let's not make this into some kind of competition. I'm not so perfect."

"You could never tell it from your grades."

"Look, I work hard, and I struggle to get the work done. Besides, we all make mistakes."

"Yes, but you make fewer than I do, and I don't have a husband or kids to distract me."

"Having a husband and kids just made me more efficient because I have to be. But you don't just sit at home doing homework all the time, you have other interests."

"You think? Well, I'll tell you, you consistently make higher grades, while you have more distractions."

"And the point is…"

"The point is I don't think you should worry about your school work suffering because you have a family."

"It was a joke!"

"And you aren't neglecting your family because you are in school. You're a great mom."

"Erica! It was only a joke. I was trying to get you riled up."

"So you say. But I've watched you stress out. I think you said what you really feel. What you keep hidden deep down inside."

"And I think you've been taking too many psychology classes."

"You're a great mom and a hard-working student. No one could ask for more."

"And you, Erica, are a fantastic friend. You are right, I have been worrying about my decision to continue with school."

"I knew it!"

"So thanks for the encouragement. I appreciate it."

"Yeah, well, I'm hiding my jealous tendencies well."

"What do you mean? I might luck out and make the occasional higher grade, but you make great grades. And besides, we're not in a competition. What do you have to be jealous about?"

"Grades, schmades. Who cares about grades?" Erica scoffed.

I looked at her in surprise. If Erica was going to try to make me believe she did not care about grades...well, the girl worked entirely too hard to not care.

I looked at my friend and realized that her crossed-arm stance reminded me of that of a stubborn three year old. I knew exactly how to deal with three year olds. I squinted my eyes just the right amount and turned the ever-powerful "tell me the truth" beam on her.

Erica's shoulders hunched as she struggled to resist, and beads of sweat began forming on her upper lip. After several moments passed with us locked in silent battle, I noticed that her knuckles had begun to turn white.

"Okay," Erica conceded, cracking under the pressure of the Truth Beam, "I do care about grades."

I un-squinted just a bit, but kept the Truth Beam focused on my friend. I knew from past experience that a too sudden release from the power of the Truth Beam often resulted in a backlash of lies.

119

"What I am jealous of is your family," she continued quietly. "I want one of those."

"Of course you do, Erica!" I said, relieved that I had gotten to the crux of the matter and could now put away the Truth Beam. "Families are great. But you're young yet, and besides you know, you have to date to find a good guy. And how often do you take the time to go out on a date?"

"It's funny you should mention that…"

"Mention what?"

"Mention a date, silly!"

"You mean you have a date tonight?"

"Yep"

"But that's great! What are you doing sitting around here? You're done with your project, go on, get out of here."

"I would, but I have a little conflict tonight that I didn't expect."

"What is it?"

"You."

"Me?"

"Yes, you. You see, last week I was thinking about friendship, and what it means to be a good friend. I decided that a good friend wouldn't let her friend work all alone at night in a dusty, murky old basement."

"It's not dusty or murky. I'll be fine. I've been here by myself plenty of times before."

"I know you have Vanessa, but I'm getting a little nervous about it. There have been some strange things on the news lately that creep me out. I'm staying until you finish your project."

"Erica, as much as I appreciate your friendship," I said firmly, "I don't need a babysitter. Go on your date. I'll be fine."

"I want to be a good friend, so I'm staying."

"I want to be a good friend, so I want you to leave."

"Why? Won't you feel better if I'm here?"

"I won't feel better if you miss your date. I'll feel guilty."

"Guilty?"

"Yes, guilty. You don't want to make me feel guilty, do you?"

"No. So what should I do?"

"You should go on your date and enjoy it."

"Are you sure?" she said hopefully. "I mean, wouldn't a good friend stay, to make sure you're safe, and not lonely?"

"If I feel unsafe I can call security," I glanced at her and sighed loudly, "as I struggle through the next four hours of work all alone."

"I'll stay," Erica said stubbornly. "I don't want you to stay here alone for four hours. What is a date after all?"

"Erica!" I said sternly, shaking my head. "I was teasing again. You have got to recognize when someone is kidding. There are entirely too many people out there like me who think its fun. Learn the signs. Recognize them. Don't be gullible. "

"You mean you won't be lonely here by yourself?" She looked so hopeful, like a puppy waiting for its favorite treat.

"Lonely?" I asked, raising one eyebrow to make a point. "Do you remember that I live in a house bursting with children? Have you ever spent time with my daughters? A little bit of quiet time will be like a vacation."

"You want me to leave so that you can have quiet? Are you saying I talk too much?" Erica asked, crinkling her brow in consternation.

"Erica, of course not!" I said quickly. Panic-stricken thoughts raced through my mind. I knew Erica well enough to know that if she thought I thought she talked too much, she might not say another word for weeks! The last thing I wanted was for Erica to stop talking altogether because she thought I thought she was a chatterer.

"You talk just the right amount!" I hastily continued, "not too much, not too…"

The mischievous grin that spread across Erica's face stopped my words cold.

"Erica, are you…"

"Gotcha!" she crowed gleefully.

I struggled to hold down the corners of my mouth. It would not do to let Erica know how happy I was that she got it. She understood. She was now a fully initiated member in the strange and wonderful world of banter.

"As I was saying before you decided to become a jokester," I continued in a serious tone, ruthlessly interrupting Erica's gloating session, "you should go on your date. I'm a big girl and I can look out for myself."

Erica's triumphant grin slowly morphed into the thoughtful look that normally resided on her face. "If you are sure you don't mind...well, I would like to go on this date."

"So tell me about this guy," I prodded in my you-might-as-well-tell-me-everything-because-I'll-find-out-anyway voice that I used with reluctant daughters.

She cracked like an egg. Information plopped out like an oversized yolk.

"He's got brown hair, brown eyes—he's cute of course—a junior, and his major is computer science. We've been friends for a couple of years now, but this will be our official first date."

Startled by the uncharacteristic outpouring of information, I wondered if she was falling for this guy. A good friend would find out as much as possible, and I had every intention of being a good friend.

Besides, no mother in her right mind would give up the opportunity to hone her investigation skills—a mother of three needs to keep her questioning abilities razor sharp.

"Did you know him before school," I used the old tilted head trick, so the question seemed friendly rather than probing, "like in high school?"

"No," Erica responded, not the least offended by my query. "I met him my freshman year."

"Did you have a class together?"

"No, we met in the dorm."

"Do you have mutual friends? Do you have a lot in common?"

"We have a few of the same friends, but not many. What I like about him most is that he is sweet, kind, and we have a similar sense of humor. We like a lot of the same movies."

"So, do you *really* like this guy?" I probably shouldn't have jumped straight to *the* question, but I did not feel that subterfuge was needed. Erica was happy I was interested. She wanted to talk.

"I'm not sure yet," she said, staring off into space.

Relieved, I decided that this inquisition did not need to be quite as intense as I had first supposed. She was in no imminent danger of falling head over heals in love.

"He's a great guy," she continued, "but until now, he's only been a friend. We'll see if it develops into a different kind of relationship."

That wait-and-see attitude relieved my fear that Erica was falling for this guy too fast. I wanted my friend to find a good guy, but not just any guy. He needed to be the right guy, and only time would tell if he was right for Erica.

"When do you need to go?" I asked as I looked at the clock and realized how much time had slipped by.

"Well, um…"

"Well, um what?"

"To be honest, I told him I couldn't go," Erica admitted sheepishly. "He said he understood, but if I changed my mind I could meet him and his friends at the Ram."

That did not sound too promising. Did this guy ask Erica out on a date, or to hang out with him and his friends?

"Erica," I asked with in what I hoped was a casual tone, "was this date supposed to be a double date or something?"

"No. It would have been a regular date, but he set it up this way to give me more flexibility since I didn't think I could go. You see if I show up, we'll go to a movie together, just the two of us. If I don't, he'll stay out with his friends."

"Why didn't he just reschedule with you? For another night?"

"He was trying to make it easy for me. He's sweet that way."

Red flags were popping up right and left in my mind, but I could not pin it down. Something was not right. But what?

I decided to back off a bit. Erica was my friend, not my daughter. My job as a friend was more to encourage than question.

"When will he be at the Ram? If you leave now, will he be there?" I encouraged.

"I think so, if I leave now. Are you sure you don't mind?" Erica questioned hopefully.

"Not in the least. Go. Have fun. Fall in love. Get married. Have a family."

"Hey, wait. This is only our first real date!"

"Yeah, well that's how it all gets started."

"There, that does it for this part," I muttered.

It was one of life's great mysteries that any person who spent several hours alone—like in a basement lab—would eventually begin to mutter, grumble, talk, or yell to herself. I was currently only at the muttering stage, and although I had at times made it to the talking phase, I had yet to actually yell.

Was there some deep, sociological, psychological, anthropological—or any logical— reason that a person needs to hear a human voice every so often?

Or maybe I have deluded myself. I hoped I was not the only one who has talked to myself, in the middle of the night, on campus, all alone, in the basement of a deserted building.

When I told Erica to go out on her date, and that I did not mind being alone, it really was not true. Not the going out on her date part. I certainly wanted her to do that. But the staying alone thing, well, when I thought about it....

A shiver raced down my spine as I recalled the many horror movies I had watched in my life. Each film began the same way, with a woman working all alone in a remote location, far from other reasonable human beings. Why she was all alone did not matter, not to the psycho that happened along to create a horrible and bloody tragedy.

Goose bumps covered my arms as I shuddered at the gruesome pictures floating through my head. I had to get my mind off of horror movies and back on my project. The sooner I completed it, the sooner I could go home.

Another shudder enveloped me as I realized that creepy was the most accurate word to describe the ambience of this basement at two o'clock in the morning.

I would have slapped myself to regain control but I did not like pain. Instead I decided to ignore that disturbing feeling I had that I was isolated, that there was no one left in the world except me and my goose bumps.

What right had I to feel all alone anyway? Surely if I walked outside right now I would find the campus teaming with students, professors, tourists, janitors, security guards, gardeners, administrators, and all the other people who made the campus like a city rather than a university.

Oh, right. It was the middle of the night, and all those people were snug in their own beds sleeping like all the rest of the sane people.

With that thought, I gave up. It was evident I had distracted myself beyond the point of no return. There was no hope I would get anything else accomplished in those wee hours of the morning. It was time to hang up my hat, to hit the road, to get out of Dodge. Or at least gather up my purse, my papers, and my—

"What the heck?" I said.

There I went, talking to myself again.

But this time it was vindicated. I had been startled into speech by the strange humming sound that was coming from the hallway.

The hallway that should have been deserted at this time of night. The hallway I needed to traverse in order to leave the creepy basement and head home to my nice, safe, well-populated house.

I sighed as I watched the second hand of my wristwatch make its tortuously slow circuit around the dial.

Patience was not really one of my virtues, but maybe, just maybe, I could outwait that worrisome humming noise.

Once the second hand had completed two agonizingly slow circuits I allowed myself a little sigh. After it had done four more leisurely strolls around the dial, I was discouraged beyond measure—the humming continued unabated.

"Darn it, this is ridiculous. I'm so tired I don't care if psychos or alien are lurking outside the door ready to pounce. I'm going home, and I'm going home now."

My hope was that the way the hum sounded like it originated from within the building, right outside the lab, was an aural illusion. I longed to discover that it emanated from some distant location, far, far, away—in the opposite direction from my lonely little car that waited for me in the dark and lonely parking lot.

It was peculiar how often the word "lonely" popped into my head. Probably because being truly alone was one of my nightmares. I would not survive long without other humans. I was a social being.

Bravely I gathered my belongings, disregarding the fear I felt of what I might find outside the door. I was no longer willing to remain trapped in the lab. Straightening my shoulders I boldly marched to the door and flipped off the light switch. As my hand touched the knob my nerve left me, and I exhibited extreme caution as I gingerly eased open the lab door. All hope that the hum that droned on and on originated from outside the building was squashed immediately. The noise, which had been an annoying buzz with the door closed, escalated dramatically as I cracked the door a mere half inch. The hum now filled the room with a pulsating throb, at least ten times louder than before.

Gathering my courage I began to widen the gap, only to be frozen in shock—for coming out of what I had assumed was the janitor's closet directly opposite the lab was the most bizarre assortment of weirdos I had ever seen.

I called them weirdos because it was evident they had no business in the building at that time of night, and who except weirdoes hung out in a creepy basement at two a.m. if they did not need to? I needed to be here, but I did not want to be. What were they doing in the basement of Denny Hall at that time of night?

Not one of the ten (I counted) oddly garbed people directed a look my way. They just exited the basement quietly, with no talking, no sighs, no mutters, no coughs, and no eye contact with each other.

I shivered as I realized how like robots they appeared. They dressed in a freakish mode, but had none of the normal (if you could call it normal) mannerisms of the freaks found wandering around the university district.

And again I had to ask myself, why were they in this building? At two a.m.?

I heard the outer door gently latch and could plainly see that the hallway was now empty. The weirdos had left the building.

I gently closed the door to think. Was it safe to leave? What would happen if I took a chance and made a break for it?

At that moment, movement outside the windows caught my eye. One by one, in single file, the group walked past the lab windows, allowing me the opportunity to count them. All ten were accounted for. It was safe to leave. I only needed to be careful once I left the building that I did not run into the strange group before I could safely reach my car.

I carefully inched the lab door open again. No one was in sight, and the humming noise had stopped. It was safe to leave the creepy basement which was truly a perfect scenario for a horror flick.

As I tiptoed near the janitor's closet, I paused in thought. How, I wondered, did ten people fit into that tiny, little janitor's closet? What would draw them to such a strange place for a freak meeting?

The door had been left slightly ajar. I had never seen it open before—I was pretty sure the door has always been kept locked.

One quick peek and I would head for home.

Chapter 12

"WHERE THE HECK AM I?"

It was a silly question really, as I could plainly see that I was in the middle of a gigantic, warehouse-style lab. Or was it a lab-style warehouse?

Scurrying around like rats in a maze were hundreds of men and women in white coats, darting about from location to location, sometimes in groups, and sometimes singly.

Whoever decorated the lab must have believed that the best work environment lacked distracting colors and vowed to keep those nasty distractions out to the way. The only color visible was white. White tables, white walls, white ceiling, white chairs...well, you get the picture. If the sterile look was what they wanted, this room was a flaming success!

And here I sat, in my jeans and bright red sweater, an obvious spot of color in the otherwise colorless room. I was a blue and red boat, floundering alone in an endless white sea. I was a butterfly fluttering in a snow-covered field, a single Fruit Loop floating in a bowl of milk.

Yet it would appear that no one had noticed me for at least two hours.

It was surreal. It was bizarre. It was unsettling. I had never before felt so uncomfortably invisible.

I could only imagine that it was an experiment conducted by a brilliant, though unscrupulous, scientist who wanted to see how long a person would patiently wait while surrounded by a room full of people who totally ignored her.

Little did the scientist know that I was not the best subject for the experiment. By my calculations it must have been at least four or five o'clock in the morning, which meant the girls would be waking up soon. Tony had a test in his morning class and could not miss it. I had just had an unbelievably long day, on top of which I had waited patiently in this colorless room for someone to talk to me for over two hours. I was exhausted and cranky. I needed to go home.

It was time for this experiment to end. I had been here long enough. I had already contributed two hours of my time to further Science.

Besides, patience was not one of my strong suits.

"Hello," I sang out in my most pleasant voice, "may I speak to someone for a moment?" Cranky or not, it probably was wise to try to make friends with these people. Good manners usually helped.

Not one person so much as paused a step. The rats continued to bustle around the maze.

"I would like to talk to a supervisor," I said again loudly, careful to keep my voice out of the panicked or obnoxious range.

Not a single head turned in my direction. Maddening, truly maddening. Did they not understand that I was trying to get their attention?

"Does anyone here speak English?" I yelled as my control slipped a bit.

The rats kept marching on and on.

"¿Hablas español?" I chirped, regaining enough composure to sound like a sane person. I had taken two years of college Spanish, not really enough to be fluent but enough to get by.

Round and round the maze they go; where they stop, nobody knows.

"Parlez-vous français?" High school French to the rescue!

Or not.

"Sprechen sie Deutsch?" This was really a stretch, since I had only take one quarter of German. If I was forced to communicate just in that language; I'd be up the proverbial creek without a paddle.

Not a blink, not a waiver from their chosen path. It was almost as if they could neither see nor hear me.

What was going on here? Had I entered the Twilight Zone? Was there a force field around me? Or maybe I was in a room totally inhabited by people who were both blind and deaf. Or zombies! These rats-in-a-maze people did share characteristics with some zombies I had seen in old movies.

Time to get a grip before my imagination truly got the better of me. I simply had to remember that these were normal people, doing normal jobs—a little hard of hearing and shortsighted perhaps, but normal nonetheless.

Since the soft approach had had no effect, it was time to take off the kid gloves.

I opened my mouth to really make some noise, when my stomach began its own cacophony of sound, which reminded me that I had forgotten to eat dinner.

The thought of food would have made my mouth water, except I was too dehydrated. If I did not get something to drink soon, it was quite possible my lips would dry up and blow away.

I had to restructure my plan of attack. What I needed was a focused target. I had to find the person most likely to listen to me, most likely to sympathize.

But a bad case of cotton mouth was really beginning to distract me. Even before I found someone to let me out, I needed water. Then I would work on my escape.

I scanned the huge white room, hoping to catch sight of a water fountain. Nothing even remotely resembling one was anywhere in sight. But as I looked around I noticed something odd, very odd.

"It must be my imagination," I muttered as I watched the lab workers scurrying around, "these people seem to be not so much ignoring me, as going out of their way to avoid me."

Mystified, I watched as a woman walked down a passageway toward me, pause a few feet away, turn to her right, walk several feet, turn to her left, walk several more feet, turn to her left again, walk several feet again, and end up in a spot she could have reached in a quarter of the time if she had just taken a straight path past me.

"It's like I'm in an invisible ten-by-ten-foot box." I said. Then I yawned and shrugged my shoulders.

"Right now, I just don't give a hoot. I'm exhausted, ravenous, and parched. I'm also sick to death of these people torturing me this way. When are they going to let me go?"

I looked around at the rats scurrying about, minding their own business, ignoring my presence, making me stay awake when I wanted to sleep, letting me sit here hungry and thirsty, keeping me prisoner—

For all I knew these lab rats might not even know of my discomfort. It was time I let them know I had had enough. My momma did not raise a wimp. I needed to take action!

"Excuse me, ma'am," I said, trying to get the attention of the woman who had so carefully avoided my space. "Ma'am, I'm talking to you—hey you, in the white coat."

Of all the idiotic things to say! Everyone was wearing a white coat. I decided to ignore my blunder and focus all my efforts on getting the woman to look my way.

"Excuse me, please look over here," I pleaded. "I really need to talk to you for just a minute."

The woman did not so much as flinch, pause, or even blink. Well, honestly I could not tell about the blinking part, since she was determined to keep her back to me. She just calmly continued about her business as if she had not heard I word I said.

Or as if she had no clue I even existed!

Whoever these people were, they needed a training session on manners. Guests should never be treated as shabbily as I was being treated.

Realizing that my current frustration level might cause me to lose *my* manners, I paused a moment to take a couple of slow, deep breaths. When I felt I had myself under control again, I hopped out of my chair and moved toward the woman.

My sudden movement had no effect on her whatsoever. Shouldn't she at least glance my way, if only to assure herself that I was not about to collide with her?

I detested being ignored this way. Overlooked, disregarded, shunned! This behavior had gone on long enough. If they were going to keep me here, the least they could do was show me some common courtesy. A drink of water would be a good start.

"Hey, listen up," I began again, addressing the woman in white. "All I want is a little glass of water. I won't bother you again if you just tell me where I can get a drink."

It was like talking to a brick wall.

"Look here, lady," I said more firmly.

I really was not all that surprised when she did not look.

It was time for stronger tactics. I would invade her space—make her look me in the face. It was much harder to rudely ignore someone who was an inch from your nose, sharing your breathing space.

I hoped I did not have bad breath.

Even more, I hoped she did not.

I took three steps toward my intended victim before I clumsily tripped over a chair. Lucky for me, my fall was short.

Strangely short. Instead of plummeting several feet to the floor, I only dropped a couple of inches before I was abruptly halted by an invisible barrier.

The odd thing was that the barrier did not feel in the least like a wall. Where it should have been hard, it was soft. Instead of the expected coldness, I found it pleasantly warm. It was rather like the way luxurious mattresses made a person feel she was sleeping on clouds.

As tired as I was right then, I felt the urge to curl up against the wall and take a little nap. It would be much more comfortable than the cold, hard table I had been sitting at for hours.

Sanity reasserted itself as a loud growl from my stomach prompted my brain to recall that I was at the point of starvation. Determination returned as the sound of my sandpaper lips grating against each other nudged my thirst back into the forefront of my thoughts.

As tired as I was, I was not going to give up and go to sleep. I needed to get out of this place and go home.

In order to get out of my invisible box, I first needed to explore it. Placing my hands flat against the warm, pillow-like surface, I carefully traversed around the box, checking high and low to see the exact dimensions of my prison. I was rather pleased to find that my first instinct was correct. My padded cell was pretty much the size of a single dorm room, ten feet by ten feet.

"Now that I've checked the sides," I whispered, "I'd better check the ceiling. It would be good to know how much air I have in this box.

Climbing onto the table, I reached overhead. Before I had even straightened my arms fully they were halted by the strange pillow-like substance.

I'm ashamed to say I panicked a bit at that point. I tried, I really tried, but no force on earth could hold back the hysterical giggle that erupted from my mouth.

"A mime," I yelled in hysteria. "I've become a mime in an invisible padded cell!"

Ashamed at my outburst, I burst into tears as I climbed down from the table. I was humiliated and defeated. What an idiot I must have looked to the rats scurrying around the lab.

Unless...

I pulled myself together, threw back my head, and let out the loudest, most bloodcurdling scream I could muster.

I looked around at the co-occupiers of the giant lab. It was obvious that my scream had had no effect whatsoever. Was this a soundproof cell?

I remembered as a child the sound of other children playing outside while I tried to nap. Their shrill voices flowed freely through the open window, but my mother was successful in providing a quiet environment for my nap by the simple expedient of closing all the doors, windows, and curtains.

What she could not do, however, was keep out the sound of nearby construction. I laid there for a full hour, unable to block out the fascinating low-pitched sound of metal on wood.

141

I did not have any metal to strike with, but I did have my hand. I reached out my hand and moved forward until I once again found a wall. Standing a mere foot away, I drew back my fist and swung with all my might. I was determined that the sound of my fist on the wall would be heard throughout the lab, startling a reaction from all those going about their business as if they did not know I existed.

As my fist approached the point of impact I cringed in expectation of pain. This was really going to hurt.

I might as well have punched a marshmallow. There was no pain, but more importantly, absolutely no noise.

"Well, how do you like that!" I said in disgust. "I guess I could yell all I wanted and never get a response."

I stood still for a moment, deep in thought. Then I climbed back up on the table.

"You might not be able to hear me," I yelled defiantly, "but I bet you can see me just as well as I can see you."

My plan was to move about as much as possible, and as randomly as I could manage. Erratic movement was most likely to capture attention.

I began by flapping my wings up and down like a giant bird frantically trying to take flight. Then I progressed to randomly spaced jumps combined with flailing arms.

looked like a deranged pelican, but
lmly walked on. No one even glanced
ion.

rated, I did my version of Riverdance,
ny arm pits as I leapt about like a
ed, thrashed about, and screamed
asure until I was thoroughly

worked. No matter how
d, there was no response. I could
had to accept that no one could see

Tired and frustrated, I admitted defeat. I was truly invisible. No matter much hunger and thirst I felt, I had no recourse but to wait.

With a sigh, I curled up in a fetal position and leaned against the spongy velvet that formed my prison walls. At least there was one benefit of being trapped in a soundproof room, the walls made terrific pillows.

As I yawned, I knew without a doubt that I would at least escape from one discomfort—sleep deprivation. Whether my dreams would be good ones or bad ones—well, that remained to be seen.

I awoke to the sound of whispering.

I was still extremely tired, so I decided to ignore the whisperers and stay in my comfortable position on the floor, leaning against the giant pillow that was my prison. It served the men right if they never caught on that I was no longer asleep.

143

I did not feel it was wrong to eavesdrop when it came to the victim overhearing the plans of her jailers. Besides, if they were really concerned I might hear too much about their dastardly plot, shouldn't they hold their little confab outside of my cell?

"Are you sure," a male voice asked softly yet sternly, "that you can safely do it again?"

"Yes, yes, yes," a second male voice responded. "Just like I told you. There should be no problems if I shield her a second time. She'll have no ill effects."

"No ill effects! Do you not think that her forgetting her family was an ill effect?"

"I know, I know. That was a mistake. But there was no harm done, no permanent damage."

"There had better be no permanent damage. We need her alive and well."

"Don't worry, I know what the mistake was."

"Good, because she needs to remember that she is pregnant. Much better for the baby."

"What?" I yelled, shocked into betraying that I was awake. I jumped up so quickly I did not notice that one of my legs had fallen asleep. I barely had become upright before I began my descent toward the floor.

Fortunately one of the whispering men was a quick thinker and grabbed my arm, saving me from a potentially painful tumble to the floor. He looked slightly embarrassed. Did it bother him that I had overheard his conversation?

Frankly, I did not care!

"What did you say about a baby?" I demanded, furiously shaking my arm to dislodge the man's hand. The man continued to grip my arm as he sent a quick glare at the other man.

"You are pregnant with your fourth daughter," he answered politely as he turned in my direction. "Congratulations."

"Thank you for the congratulations," I said, staring pointedly as my arm, "but I would appreciate it if you would not leave a bruise. I can stand perfectly well on my own now."

Confused, the man looked down at his hand, which had a death grip on my arm, and quickly let go. It appeared that in his distraction he had forgotten that he was holding it.

"Now," I continued, rubbing my throbbing arm, "you said something about me forgetting I was pregnant just like I had forgotten my family."

"That's right," the man said, and I was pretty sure I detected a trace of guilt in his voice.

"I remember the forgetting my family incident, but I don't recall *ever* knowing that I was pregnant."

The man looked at me and swallowed. I watched in amazement as his face began to flush red. Why was he blushing?

"I deserve an explanation," I stated firmly. An offensive assault was often the best defense.

"You've been here before, " the man began, but he got no further before he had to stop to clear his throat.

I waited a few seconds, but the man showed no sign of continuing. "Go on, I'm listening," I prompted.

"We sent you back home after shielding your memories. Only we...," his face turned beet red, "I made a mistake and shielded a few extra memories. Some of them important ones."

"A few extra memories? *You* made me forget my family?"

The man nodded his head. I still did not know what was going on, but one look at the shame on this man's face kept me from feeling threatened. True villains could never succeed if they had this much conscience.

"Let's begin at the beginning," I suggested calmly. "Where is 'here'?"

"Physically," the man said, pausing a moment to bite his lower lip, "'here' is the University of Washington."

I looked around. It felt like a university lab, but I was not buying it. A lab this large would not have escaped my notice for the last three years. I was not getting the full story.

Something about his choice of words and that little bite of the lower lip jogged a memory. I saw in my mind's eye my daughter Becca, telling me she had eaten every fish stick on her plate. When I cleared the table I found a napkin full of fish sticks. I confronted my daughter with her lie, only to be informed by the potential future lawyer that she had told only the truth. The fish sticks were in her napkin, no on her plate.

I was going to have to ask a lot of very precise questions if I wanted to get to the truth.

"Where in the University of Washington?"

"Well—"

"What building?"

"I, um—"

"What department owns this lab?"

"You see—"

"This is a very large lab that could not easily be hidden, especially with this huge number of people working in it. Why have I never seen or heard of this lab before?"

The man did not even try to answer. He just stood there with a pained expression plastered on his face, discomfort oozing from every pore.

"Would you like a chair?"

The voice came from behind me, and I turned to see that the second man had stepped forward and pulled a chair out from the table. The first man looked as if he had just been told that plans had been changed and he would not be required to jump off of a mile high cliff after all.

"Will I need a chair?" I questioned.

"It probably would be wisest if you take a seat before we continue this discussion," the man answered kindly.

Chapter 13

"MOMMY, WHAT ARE YOU DOING!" my daughter yelled as I pulled on a sweater.

I sighed, and not for the first time. Becca had just begun a new phase, one that I could not wait for her to outgrow. A few days ago she had suddenly decided that her goal in life was to make her mother fashionable. To do this, she had become a personal fashion expert—for me. Every time I put on a piece of clothing, she commented on it, usually negatively.

Her enthusiasm knew no bounds. If this was not so much a phase as a sign that Becca had made an early decision about her career choice, the fashion industry could look forward to a tireless worker with an eagle eye among their ranks.

Ranks? No, I misspoke. With her passion she would not be in the ranks for long. She was destined to be a leader in the fashion industry, coercing all to her will, humiliating all who could not see her vision, transforming the world of fashion forever.

That was my prediction, and I was going to stick with it. After all, what else could I envision while dealing with a child who transformed from a loving daughter to a fashion tyrant. I cringed at the thought of accidentally mismatching my clothing in the smallest degree. You would think I was committing an act of treason!

"I'm getting dressed, darling. Mommy gets dressed every day, and has every day since she was born." I was using my best mommy voice, trying to calm the irrational fashion fears of this budding designer.

"But that's not right. It doesn't go like that."

"What doesn't go like what, sweetie?"

"That sweater. It doesn't go like that."

"Sweetheart, I think I know how a sweater goes. I've been wearing them for years."

"No, Mommy. You're wrong."

The shock was almost too much to bear—my wonderful, lovely, usually respectful eight year old was turning into a know-it-all teenager right before my eyes.

What had gone wrong? How could this be happening to me? So early too!

Just last week she was asking me which color to use for the elephants in her coloring book. This week she suddenly knew all the nuances of which shade of red could be properly worn with royal blue.

Most horrid of all was that like a teenager, she would not let it go. Every day this week, she would not let me leave my bedroom until she approved of my attire.

I'll admit that at first I thought it was cute. Now...well, now it was getting very old, very fast. It was time to put a stop to it.

"My darling child," I began, moving to the bed so that I could sit on the edge. This would be a more effective conversation if I refrained from towering over the child. "I'm thirty-two years old, and you are only eight. I think my thirty-two years of dressing gives me the knowledge I need to know how to wear clothes. Do you think your eight years makes you an expert?"

"Mommy, you're getting dressed all funny. And besides, I'm nine."

"Almost nine. And what do you mean all funny? Don't you like my clothes?"

"No, Mommy, I don't. Your socks are on all wrong. And you are putting the sweater on wrong-side out. And your pants are on backwards. And none of the colors match."

I sat in silence as this litany of complaints poured forth. What was happening to my child, that the world looked so mixed?

"And Mommy," Becca sniffled, tears streaming down her cheeks, "you don't look like you!"

"Oh darling, come here!" I threw my arms around her shoulders and pulled her to me. A child going through this sort of internal struggle needed a hug.

It was time for me to stand up and be a mom. No one said it would be easy, or pain free. If it helped my child to give me fashion advice every morning as I dressed, so be it. It would not be forever. I only needed time to figure out what was bothering Becca and help her solve her problem.

I should find some time to talk to Becca's teacher to see if anything had changed in her classroom. I'd read that these changes in behavior were often caused by simple things like a new classroom novel, or learning about an upsetting event in history, or a new kid who was bossy, or… who knew what. There had to be a change at school that upset my daughter and made her act this way!

I hugged my daughter again and said, "Don't worry darling, it will be okay. Just go ahead and tell me how I should wear my clothes."

"I have been telling you, all week," Becca said, pulling out of my arms. "I'm tired of telling you. You should just wear them the right way. This isn't funny."

Confused, I looked at my daughter, standing there with her arms crossed, a most unusual frown marring her normally cheerful face.

"But darling," I said soothingly, "I'm not trying to be funny. I have been wearing my clothes the right way."

Becca took a step away from me, and I was surprised to see the frown on her face replaced by fear.

"Mommy, are you sick, or are you joking?"

"Neither, sweetie."

"It's okay, Mommy," Becca said gently, her shoulders tensing up as if she expected a blow, "I know parents can get sick if they have too much stuff to do. Do you have too much stuff to do?"

"Oh sweetie," I cried, "my life is wonderful and fun and perfect! I have just the right amount of stuff to do."

"I could learn how to cook," my sweet angel suggested tentatively, "and that would help you get better. If you did not have to cook dinner, you would have more time to..." her voice trailed off in confusion.

"To do what, darling?"

"I don't know, Mommy...to remember how to put your clothes on right?"

"Becca, I haven't forgotten how dress myself."

"Yes you have Mommy," the confusion dissipated as the stubborn stance was immediately resumed, crossed arms, tapping foot and all, "and I don't understand. You taught me how to dress. How could you forget?"

"Sweetie, I haven't forgotten. We are just disagreeing. The way I am dressing is perfectly fine, but you just don't like it."

My daughter turned around, walked a few feet away, and turned back to me to give me the once over, never once uncrossing those stubborn arms. I wish I knew what was going on in that brain of hers.

She stood for a few seconds looking at me, and then she seemed to come to a decision. With a sigh she walked over to the dresser and uncrossed her arms just long enough to pick up the digital camera that rested there.

"No, Mommy, I'm not disagreeing," she stated firmly as she struggled to re-cross her arms while holding the camera. After a few futile attempts she gave up and just held the camera tightly to her chest. "You are dressed all wrong. And yesterday you were all wrong. And the day before you were all wrong. And if I hadn't helped you, you would have left the house all funny. I think you must be sick."

"I'm not sick! And my darling child, what makes you say that everything is all wrong?"

She looked darling standing there, stern and serious. I could not hide the smile that spread across my face. I opened my arms for a hug.

In her eight-year-old wisdom, she simply shook her head and walked out of the room.

"Daddy, Zoe, Maddie, can you come here a minute? Mommy needs you," I heard my daughter call.

"Sure, sweetie," my husband responded from another room, "I'll be right there. Where are you?"

"Mommy's bedroom."

Becca stepped back into the room. She looked at me a moment and then walked over, grabbed my hands and pulled me off the bed where I had been sitting.

"Okay, Mommy, I want you to stand right here. I want to take a picture of you."

"You certainly have been taking a lot of pictures of my lately."

"It's evidence."

What was this child up to?

In less than a minute my seven year old, Maddie, had joined us. She took one look at me and giggled.

Zoe, the youngest, came in just a few moments later. The little munchkin looked at me and grinned. "Mommy's a clown, mommy's a clown," she began to chant.

The complexity of the three-year-old brain was unfathomable. What could I possibly be wearing to trigger the image of a clown in her head?

At that moment, my husband entered the room and smiled.

I knew I something was wrong when he winked at me and said, "Well girls, isn't your mother a fashion plate today. Becca, did you pick out your mother's oh-so-stylish outfit?"

"No way," Becca said in an offended voice.

"Ah, so your mother came up with this outfit all on her own? Without your artistic eye? Very good, honey. I think you've outdone yourself."

It was too much for me. My husband obviously thought I had dressed funny to entertain the children. My children thought I looked like a clown.

I was simply trying to get dressed for the day. I sat back on the bed and put my hands up to my face.

"What's the matter, honey?" my husband asked. "I thought you did a great job. It is a very funny outfit."

I could not help myself. I burst into tears. Immediately I felt three sets of little hands and one big set pat me on the back and shoulders.

"It's okay, Mommy," the littlest voice said. "we'll make boo-boo better."

For some reason that only made me cry harder.

* * *

I could not stop crying, and I cried for hours. I did not know exactly what was wrong with me, but I was absolutely certain I must be losing my mind.

Becca had shown us all the "evidence" she had collected on the digital camera. My husband had smiled at every photo, and my two younger girls had giggled. They all thought it was some big joke Becca and I had cooked up. An elaborate ruse meant to entertain.

I would have felt humiliated, except for Becca. She was in her protective mode and kept mum that I had not a clue. It was fantastic when a child showed a parent such wonderful instincts.

Because in reality, if I were truly honest, I would have to admit that I did not know what the giggles and guffaws were about. I could not see a thing wrong with any of the outfits.

Becca tried her best to help me understand. She brought me magazines and showed my how other people dressed. I could see that most people did not wear their sweaters on their lower half, like I had tried to do yesterday. But it had looked good to me, and it had been very soft and comfortable.

I was surprised that I could not find a single picture of a person with socks on their hands—a style I had tried out the day before yesterday. Becca was horrified, but I could not see any difference between socks and gloves. In my eyes, there was very little difference.

Just as there was no difference between a woolen cap and a pair of tights—except the tights fit better on my head and enhanced the look of my outfit.

But Becca was so upset, and so protective, that I knew something had to be wrong with me.

So I told my husband I had a horrible headache, skipped my classes, and lay in bed, sobbing, and worrying.

Every hour or so, my husband poked his head into the room to check on me.

Eventually he would discover that the cogs in my brain had slipped. What then? How would he react to the knowledge that instead of brain power, I was functioning on crazy power? I'd lost my marbles and did not know where to find them. I was one card short of a full deck. I...I...I must stop this nonsense. All the sayings in the world would not make the situation any better.

Then I had a horrible thought. What if he took the kids and deserted me because he wanted to protect his children from a crazy woman?

But maybe I was worrying unnecessarily. Tony might have been playing along with Becca, and he might not really agree with her judgment that I had dressed crazily. Maybe Becca was just too immature to understand the sense of my selections?

Besides, did dressing funny mean that I was crazy?

Was I crazy?

Was I a danger to my kids?

The thought that I might be a danger to my children made me cry harder than ever. I finally gave up trying to think through the situation and cried myself to sleep.

I awoke from my nap feeling not only revived, but lighter—as if a weight had been lifted from my shoulders, and from my mind.

Everything was clearer. I had been functioning in a fog before, and now the fog had been blown away by the fresh winds of sleep.

I rolled my eyes at the thought of such foolishness. Fresh winds of sleep indeed!

I now felt like my old self again, eager for a challenge and ready to face the world. And the first challenge I needed to tackle was to figure out if my daughter had any valid reasons to dislike my style of dress.

Bracing myself for whatever was to come I grabbed the digital camera off the dresser and sat back down on the bed. I scrolled through the pictures of my children playing with a neighbor's dog, building cities in our living room, and making faces while they crammed more birthday cake than was physically possible into their mouths. Finally I came to the photos Becca had taken of my "outfits."

"Oh my goodness," I whispered, stunned by what I saw. "I didn't slip a cog. I went stark, raving mad!"

The respect I felt for my eight, almost nine-year-old daughter skyrocketed dramatically. The way she had maintained her cool and kept my craziness from her father was astounding, and come to think of it, rather scary.

Now that I had returned from the Land of Delusion, I could plainly see what had concerned my daughter. My clothing choices showed an irrefutably unbalanced mind—sickeningly unbalanced.

Most of the outfits I had dressed myself in would have made a bag lady look at me askance, though she might have asked to borrow the oh-so-stylish hat I had donned as a shoe a few days ago.

I gulped. If it had not been for the caring heart of my lovely little daughter I might not be here. If I had left the house to go to class…well, the bus driver would have felt compelled to call the guys in the white coats with the straight jacket to cart me away for the protection of society. I would have been locked up for life.

What a scary thought, that a person's mind could slip without that person having a clue that anything was wrong. I had not recognized that the slightest problem existed.

Perhaps even scarier was the realization that my smart, usually observant husband had been so easily fooled. He had let a mad woman roam around unattended for days, tending to his children without oversight—my children.

Scariest of all was that I had been saved from myself by the quick thinking of an eight-year-old girl. A girl who had only learned how to tie her shoes a few years earlier.

I might as well go ahead and wrap the car in Styrofoam, clear the streets, and teach the girl to drive. It was the inevitable next step.

Chapter 14

"DID YOU HEAR?" ERICA ASKED excitedly, just as I arrived in the basement lab of Denny Hall.

The excitement on Erica's face was obvious and alien, rather like a single sunflower towering in a field of moss. You could not miss it if you tried, but it just did not look right somehow.

Frankly, Erica's usual understated emotional response drove me batty. I vowed to get her out of her minimalist habit and into one that showed the world that she was a real girl, not a robot. I made it a rule to tease, tell tall tales, promote urban legends, and even sometimes tickle, just to encourage stronger responses. But even with all my efforts, stoic was still a good word for her; it was a given that at least one of her parents was part statue.

So if she was this emotionally charged, if I could actually see emotion on her face, it must be big. Even bigger than big—colossal, mammoth, gargantuan even!

"Did he propose?" I asked grabbing her hands, wildly guessing that her dream of getting married and starting a family was about to finally come true.

"Huh?" Erica suddenly looked confused. What a day, another emotion! The world must have shifted in its orbit. "Did who propose what?"

"The guy—the one that you deserted me in the lab to go on a date with the other night—did he get on his knees, or gaze into your eyes, or hold your hands, or even email you to propose marriage? Did he pledge his undying love to you, kiss you madly, and ask you to spend your life with him? Did he ask you to marry him?"

I suddenly realized I had never seen Erica blush before. I was fascinated to note that she was one of those fortunate people who did not become blotchy and awkward. Instead, her pale face came alive with the addition of a little color. She was suddenly very pretty.

She should blush more often. Or she should learn to replicate the effect with makeup.

I had decided to make time for a quick lesson on blush-work—the additional color was too good for her to pass up—when I realized that this was not an "I'm embarrassed" blush, it was a more "I'm furious" one. There was no doubt the earth had shifted on its axis because Erica never got mad. Major trouble was brewing on the horizon.

"Don't mention his name to me ever again!" Erica growled, and amazingly, the pink in her cheeks intensified.

"I didn't mention his name," I calmly replied, letting go of her hands and stepping back a few steps. I had never seen her angry, and I did not know if she would lose control and take her vitriol out on me. "I don't even know it."

"Good," Erica said rolling her eyes and grimacing, "that should make it easier for you to never mention him again. Ever."

"I'll agree to wipe him from my memory and never let any mention of him pass my lips on one condition."

"What?"

"You tell me why! What happened?"

Erica looked at me for a full minute before she responded. "Pull up a stool," she finally snapped, "I think I need to sit for this."

I grabbed two stools and placed them at our regular lab table. We would be comfortable enough for a cozy chat, and if anyone came in, they would think we were doing our usual work and leave us alone.

I waited for Erica to begin, but she just sat there staring into space. Her face kept changing between the pretty pink color that I thought meant anger, to a blanched white that I assumed meant either embarrassment or humiliation.

"Okay, we're sitting," I prodded. "Can you tell me what happened to upset you so much?"

"Well, I went to the Ram like he and I had agreed."

"Yes?"

"And he was there with his friends."

"Okay, so far, so good."

"And his date."

"What! He brought a date to your date. What kind of guy is this?"

"It seems it wasn't a date at all—at least not in the conventional sense of the word. He and his two buddies had each been bragging—each thought they were the most attractive to the opposite sex—and they decided they needed to figure out once and for all who was the hunkiest. So they came up with a bet. The winner was the man who was able to convince the most women to meet him at the Ram. I was just one of twenty-three women that thought they were meeting him for a date."

"Wait," I interrupted in shock, "your guy convinced twenty-three women to meet him?"

"Yes, plus his real date, who I found out has been dating him for two years."

"Two years! And she was okay with this bet?"

Erica shrugged her shoulders. "She just smiled a lot. I guess it made her feel she was special, because she had the guy that so many women wanted."

"What about the other guys? Did they bring real dates?"

"No. Neither of them have regular girlfriends."

"I'm not surprised. So how many women showed in all, not counting your guy's regular girlfriend?"

"There were fifty-five of us pathetic women there."

"Wait a minute Erica," I said sternly, "you women weren't the pathetic ones. There is nothing wrong with going on a date with a guy you think you might be interested in. The pathetic ones are the guys, who evidently don't know that women are real people who should be treated with respect."

"I guess you're right," Erica said with a sigh.

"You know," I said thoughtfully, "I think I feel the most sorry for your guy's date."

"Really?" Erica's face once again showed confusion. She was very off balance today.

"Yes. The rest of you honestly thought you were going on a date. She must have known what was going on."

Erica rolled her eyes again. "Yes, but she went along with it."

"Right," I said emphatically, "which is why I feel sorry for her. She has dated this guy for two years, so she either knows he's a jerk and feels she can't do better, or she is so naïve that he can pull the wool over her eyes about anything. Either way, I wouldn't want to be in her shoes!"

"Good point," Erica said, as she nodded her head and allowed the corners of her mouth curve up into a small smile. Humans always felt a little less humiliated when they realized that they were not the only ones around who had been duped. Humiliation hurt less in a crowd.

I was relieved to see that her color was beginning to resume its normal hue. I let her sit for a few minutes gazing off into space, revisiting her memories in light of the new perspective.

When I felt she had her mental processes under control again, I prodded her in the ribs with my elbow. "So, now we have a restaurant crammed with fifty-five hoodwinked women. What next?"

There was no way I was going to let the story stop there. I had to know what happened when three creeps met up with a restaurant full of furious women they had mislead.

"Well," Erica continued, a rare mischievous light shining in her eyes, "at first I was furious, and fumed a bit. Then I noticed that the other women were furious too. Especially when any of us looked at the girl who was his actual date, she was gloating. Actually gloating!"

"Keep going, what happened?" I moved my stool a little closer. I wanted to hear every word, and our class was due to arrive at any time.

"I talked to a few of the other girls. They were just as mad as me. Then I noticed that our waitress seemed particularly ticked off for us. I talked to her and told her that it was my guy's party. Since he had given his credit card and started a tab, well, let's just say that his bill was quite a bit larger than expected. He had told the server that he would buy a little something for each girl who showed. Kind of a consolation prize. The little something was just much bigger than he expected."

"Good job! I hope that every month as he pays that credit card bill, he gets another twinge of guilt. Way to hit him in the wallet!"

"It won't really do any good," Erica said with another sigh.

"Why not?"

"His parents are rich. They give him everything he wants. They'll just pay off the credit card and he'll go his merry way."

"I'm sorry, Erica. It would be so much more satisfying to know he'd have to pay for years. Are you crushed that it wasn't a real date?"

"Crushed! About that guy? There is no way I would allow his actions to effect my emotions in any way. I know better than to allow a jerk, and he is a jerk, place in my busy life. He was not what I thought, and I'm just glad that I discovered his jerkiness early. Think about what it would be like to actually date a guy like that seriously."

"So what happened with—"

"I really don't want to talk about the other night any more," Erica said as she jumped off the stool and began to pace nervously. "I've closed the door on that episode and moved on. I've learned from the experience, so there is no need to revisit it again and again."

"Fair enough. So if your date isn't what you wanted to talk about…" I prompted.

I was curious, but even more, I was beginning to get seasick. First she walked in one direction for five feet, made a quick turn, and then she marched back the five feet. My eyes crossed just watching her.

"Oh right," Erica said slapping her forehead so hard she almost knocked off her glasses. I breathed a sigh of relief as she resumed her place on the stool, "I almost forgot what I wanted to tell you about! You will never guess what happened last night."

"Another date?" I asked half teasingly.

"Can you forget about my social life?" Erica said sharply, rolling her eyes for the hundredth time. "I certainly have."

"Okay, consider it forgotten. What happened last night?"

"It was a very near major disaster. All the copper wiring at the airport was stolen. The whole place had to be shut down and all the planes diverted."

"Good grief, not again! I wish someone would catch whoever is doing this."

"You mean someone has stolen copper wiring from the airport before?"

"No, not the airport. Before it was schools, and new construction. Places that are easy to get to. But airports aren't like that. Airports have security galore. How did they get into the airport undetected in the first place, much less steal something as important as the wiring? Makes you kind of scared, doesn't it?"

"'Kind of' is an understatement. Extreme fright would be more accurate."

"How did you hear about this? I watch the news all the time, and I didn't hear a word."

"Well..." Erica's blush was back, but I could tell this was not a blush of anger.

"Well what?"

"After the conversation we just had about my date I'm not sure I want to tell you." Erica's voice was barely above a mumble, and she suddenly seemed to have grown very interested in an invisible spot on the table which she was attempting to scrape off with her fingernail.

"Erica!" I said sharply. Did she really think I would allow her to not tell me?

"Well, all right. I really want to tell you about it, anyway. I have a date with a new guy who works for the airport," she said in a rush. She abandoned her excavation project and looked me full in the face. "He does something with security, so of course he knows all about this theft."

"Erica! That's great news. You need to get out away from the campus every so often."

"So," Erica said as she dropped her gaze to the table once more and resumed her excavation project, "you think it's not too soon after my date with the jerk?"

I reached over and placed my hand gently on Erica's. She stopped digging and looked up, and the pain and uncertainly in her eyes nearly killed me.

"That was not a date!" I said fiercely, vowing that if I ever met the jerk who had so callously hurt Erica, I'd slap him. Too bad I did not even know his name. It really lowered my chances of retribution.

"You even said so yourself," I continued, shifting to a milder tone. "You need to go on a real date, with a guy who will treat you right. Was this new guy reared by humans, or a pack of wolves?"

A smile slipped onto Erica's face. "I'm pretty sure he was raised by humans."

"Good, because I think the other guy was raised by hyenas. What do you know about this new guy? How did you meet him?"

"I originally met him at the wedding of my cousin years ago. He is my cousin's husband's best friend. It was really my cousin who thought it would be a good idea for us to go out."

"Wait a minute, is this the cousin who—"

"No! That cousin is in jail and not expected out for eons! The scandal of a bank robber in the family will haunt us for years."

"So this cousin—"

"Is a good cousin. She is one of the most honest and caring people you could ever meet. She has a two-year-old little girl, she volunteers at the hospital, she helps take care of her ailing grandmother, she—"

"All right, all right, I've got it. She's a wonderful person, a model citizen, and the perfect reference for any guy who takes you on a date."

"Yes," nodded Erica gravely, "as a matter of fact, she is."

"Fantastic! So when is your date?"

"Um, I know I told you that I could work tonight on our project...but...well...I mean...." Erica looked in every direction but mine.

"But, well, I mean what?" I prodded.

"Well, would you mind if I worked on our project another day?" Erica gained enough courage to look me directly in the eyes, and the intense pleading I saw there was almost overwhelming.

"Of course I—" I began.

"You see," she interrupted quickly, her words spilling from her mouth in a nervous flood, "tonight is his night off, and I can easily work on the project tomorrow night. It's not due until next week."

"I don't mind!" I reassured her. "But I'm still going to work on it tonight. I can't change my schedule, because Tony is flying out tomorrow night and will be gone almost a week. For me, it's tonight or nothing."

"Oh," my conscientious friend responded sadly, "so should I cancel my date and stay?"

I looked at Erica's despondent shoulders and knew that this date, for whatever reason, had acquired a status of great importance in Erica's life.

173

Who was I to put a roadblock in the way of her possible happiness?

"Are you kidding?" I said with forged gusto. It was difficult to produce sincere enthusiasm while I was leery about this new guy, the stability of Erica's emotions, and working alone in the lab. "This guy sounds wonderful, the perfect guy for you to go on a date with."

"So," Erica asked hopefully, "you don't mind if I go on the date and we reschedule?"

Erica looked like a small child who knew she had been a little bad during the year, unsure if she would be allowed to keep the beautiful Christmas present sitting just within her reach.

"No, it'll be just fine. I've worked alone before." I tried to infuse my voice with as much confidence and sincerity as I could muster.

"Great," Erica said, her face breaking out once more into an innocently sweet smile. Erica had changed in the last few days. She had grown into a new, more open young woman.

Unfortunately that also made her more vulnerable. She no longer had a two-mile-high wall to protect her emotions.

This guy had better be good to her, or I would have to hunt him down and lecture him as only a mother could lecture. I would bombard him with guilt, remind him of his manners, and maybe even serenade him with childish songs structured to teach good social behavior. I already had a rather wide repertoire, and I was very tenacious.

The guy would not have a chance. He would be bored into compliance in no time.

Much better for him if he just treated my friend right in the first place.

"I can work on it tomorrow after twelve," Erica said, startling me out of my reverie. I was so caught up in planning my possible attack that I had forgotten she was even in the room. I jumped a mile at the sound of her voice. How long had I been daydreaming? Had I missed anything else she had said?

"I can work on it tomorrow in the afternoon. I'll be done with my classes at twelve."

"I heard you the first time," I said gently, wondering why she had repeated herself.

"So you heard me all ten times I said I could work on it tomorrow afternoon? Somehow, based on the heavy glaze over your eyes, I was under the impression your thoughts were elsewhere."

"Well, my thoughts are here now," I retorted. I hated getting caught with my mind wandering. It was kind of like getting caught only half dressed, or with my hair not brushed, or with no makeup. "But I can't get together tomorrow afternoon, I'll be busy. I think I'll just stay late and work tonight."

"Are you sure? It's kind of creepy here at night." Erica's concern was real, and touching, especially in light of the obvious importance of this date.

"How would you know," I teased, hoping to erase the concern on her face, "have you ever stayed here by yourself? Even once?"

"Well, I was here until nine o'clock that one night, when—"

"Pish posh! Nine o'clock doesn't count as night, its still prime time. What I'm asking is, have you ever been here late enough that you got to see what really goes on here at night? Have you ever seen who roams the campus late in the dark, whether the moon is full or not?"

"Don't try that full moon stuff on me; I don't believe in werewolves. Besides, the only people who roam around campus at night are foolhardy students who should know better and the night crew of the Custodial Services. So don't try to tell me any different." Her words may have said she was not interested in what I had to say, but her eyes sparkled in anticipation of a juicy story or two.

"Well," I continued, lowering my voice as if I had a tremendous secret to tell, "I've stayed late quite a few times, and I'm pleased to say that I really haven't noticed that many foolhardy students roaming around in the middle of the night. But the custodial crew…"

Erica leaned forward to hear my next words. I could tell that I had her attention fully engaged.

"Well," I said thoughtfully, "let's just say that the night crew is rather...uh...well...let's just call them exceptional."

"Exceptional," Erica sighed, tilting her head to the side as she digested the word.

"Oh yes, exceptional. So exceptional that I would be shocked to see them walking about in the light of day—which explains why they have night jobs. I'm sure they can function much better without the attention they would receive if they came out to do their work during the day."

"So," Erica prompted, "what is so exceptional about them?"

"You wouldn't believe me if I told you." I said wryly, "and I'm not sure I should tell you. I'm pretty sure it's supposed to be a secret."

"A secret," Erica breathed excitedly, thoroughly caught up in my little ruse. Then more loudly she demanded, "Come on, I'm your best friend! What's the secret?"

"Sorry, Erica," I said sternly, shaking my head, "you are not my best friend. You are my second best friend. I've told you before that my best friend is my husband, and since I haven't told him about this, I certainly can't tell you."

Erica stared at me for a few moments as her brain worked on the problem at hand. I could tell the exact moment she finalized her strategy, and I sat back to enjoy the show.

"I totally understand your position," Erica said with every appearance of sincerity. "It is commendable that you feel it is important to your marriage that you share everything with your husband."

"Thank you," I said, knowing there would be more to follow.

Erica cleared her throat nervously and then continued. "But is it wise to share everything with your husband? Are there not some things that can be left unshared?"

I pasted a confused look on my face and asked, "What do you mean?"

"Well," Erica began. I could almost see the wheels of her brain spinning out of control. "Aren't there some things that don't necessarily need to be shared? I mean, I've never been married, but I bet that you don't make a point to tell Tony each and every time you cut your toe nails or wash your hair."

"You've got me there, I don't. But those things are a part of hygiene, a normal part of taking care of oneself. Tony doesn't share those mundane things with me either. But this is different, it is a secret—not hygiene." I spoke firmly. It would be more fun for Erica if she had to actually work to get the secret.

"Yes...hygiene. Okay. And do you tell Tony each time you drive the car?"

"No," I responded cautiously, wondering where she was going with her argument.

"What about television shows? Do you make sure he knows every detail about each TV show you watch?"

"Of course not! That would be silly, and it would bore him senseless."

"And what about all those books you read. Do you tell Tony about all the books?"

"Most of them."

"Oh. Well—"

"Look, Erica. Instead of trying to minutely define my marital communication parameters, you should probably just cancel your date and stick around. That way you can see for yourself why the staff is exceptional, and I won't have to tell you a secret I haven't yet told my husband." I was pleased that Erica was working hard toward her goal, but she needed more practice with quick adaptations. A little reverse psychology should do the trick.

"You want me to cancel my date?" All craftiness left Erica's face to be replaced by intense confusion. I had thrown her for a loop.

"If you want to learn the secret, you are going to have to stick around to find out for yourself. I'm *not* telling you anything I haven't told my husband." There, that should do it. I'd thrown down the gauntlet. Few people could ignore such a challenge.

Erica was no exception. A wily look quickly replaced the worried look. "So, I think I understand now. This secret, the one you won't tell because you've not told your husband, it is something that is important for your marriage. I don't blame you, I wouldn't tell either. I'll back off. I really don't want to intrude into your personal life."

"Whoa, hold on a minute," I said adamantly, surprised and pleased that the girl would turn the tables and try reverse psychology on me. "The secret has no impact on my marriage whatsoever."

"Oh, then I'm sorry to bother you," Erica continued, hanging her head with every evidence of sadness, "I get it. You don't want to tell me because you don't think I'm worthy of your trust."

I barely contained my laughter as I noticed the pointed brush across her cheek, as if to wipe away a tear. What progress! Erica had finally learned the tools of manipulation! Every girl needed to know those tools, though the wise refrained from using them except in times of great need.

I glanced up at the clock and realized how much time had slipped away. It was time to end this little ruse.

"Okay Erica, I'll tell you," I said with a sigh. "This should prove to you that I trust you, and that you are truly my friend."

Erica kept her head lowered, probably because she had not yet mastered the art of fake tears.

"I don't know how to say this. I don't know if you'll believe me. You know, on second thought, you probably should stay to see for yourself." I infused my voice with as much doubt as I could, which was hard, since what I really wanted to do was laugh.

Erica sniffed piteously and then brushed away more fake tears. "Please tell me, I will believe," she pleaded.

She raised her head to look at me, and I was surprised to glimpse real sadness in her eyes, along with actual tears. I almost felt guilty. Almost.

"Well," I began, "the first time I saw the night custodial crew I didn't believe it. If I hadn't seen with my own eyes..."

"Seen what with your own eyes?" Erica asked excitedly, her eyes beginning to glow in anticipation.

"Not what...who."

"Who?"

"Yes, who. And frankly, I'm shocked that they haven't been treated much better. They've worked so hard that really, I think they should be allowed to retire. It's not right they have to work all night. They're old."

"Retire? Old? Who is old and should be allowed to retire?"

"I remember as a little girl," I said, staring off into space as if I was seeing a distant memory, "they brought so much joy into my life. I enjoyed watching them whenever my mother would let me."

"Watching them? Are you trying to tell me that our night custodial crew is staffed with old TV stars?"

I nodded my head sadly. "Yes, TV, movies, commercials, you name it and they were there in all their glory. I think the ones on staff were the most famous of their time."

"Who—" Erica began timidly.

"I personally think they should be able to retire in grandeur, not work hard into the night while others sleep," I interrupted, as if I did not even hear Erica's question. "Though I suppose I can understand why the university decided to put them on the night shift. They would instantly be surrounded by a multitude of photographers and reporters if anyone caught wind that they are working here. It would be a fiasco."

"Who—" Erica once again began, this time more strongly.

Again I pretended not to hear her question. "I suppose they must have made bad investments. I can't think of any other reason stars of their magnitude would need to work at their age."

"Who are you talking about?" Erica demanded, no longer sounding in the least timid.

"Still, even if they did make bad investments, don't they have family who could help them out?"

"Tell me before I go crazy!" Erica yelled. All traces of the easygoing edge of expectation had been replaced by the frenzied fingers of frustration.

"What?" I asked, pretending to come out of the far away place I had been visiting in my mind.

"I said," Erica restated clearly, "just exactly who are you talking about?"

"The night custodial staff, of course, silly," I scoffed.

Erica rolled her eyes and huffed, "No, I mean who *are* the night custodial staff?"

"Didn't I tell you?"

"No, you did not."

"You know, I feel like I've been talking entirely too long. I should just get back to work."

"Please don't do this to me," Erica pleaded. "I really want to know, and I'll keep the secret."

I took a deep breath and let it out. "Okay, I'll tell you, as long as you understand the seriousness of this secret. You absolutely cannot tell anyone. Lives would be ruined if anyone in the media found out they were working here."

"You know me well enough to know that I can keep a secret."

"If you're sure, I'll tell you."

I paused a moment to take a few slow breaths, as if I had to prepare myself for a momentous announcement. I stood up and paced back and forth a few times, swinging my arms around to loosen up my shoulders. I returned to the stool, sat down, and cleared my throat a few times.

Erica was now thoroughly prepared for an earth-shattering announcement

"The nighttime custodial crew is made up of…" I stopped abruptly, as if I feared to continue.

"Go ahead!"

"Are you sure you won't tell?"

"Please just tell me. I won't breathe a word to anyone!"

"Okay, I know you won't betray my trust. The nighttime custodial crew is made up of two couples—Donald and Daisy, Mickey and Minnie."

"I don't recognize the names. What are their last names?'

"Duck and Mouse," I said somberly.

Erica took a moment to put the first and last names together and then broke into a grin.

"You sure had me going, you jokester. But did you have to carry your joke so far? I feel like I've been on a roller coaster ride."

"Serves you right," I said with a nod. "What kind of student makes a date with a major project to finish? You should be burning the midnight oil, like me."

"I know, I know. But do you blame me? I have a much freer schedule than you do. I don't have kids to take care of."

"No, I don't blame you," I replied thoughtfully. "You should be thankful, and you should take advantage of your free status."

"Free status! I thought you loved having a family. Do you wish you didn't?"

"Honestly, no. Having a family might make it a little harder at times, but every day I have three extra reasons to get out here and do my best. Can you imagine me trying to explain to my eight year old why she should study hard and do well in school, if I'm not doing the same?"

"I wouldn't even want to try."

"Neither would I."

"I was only teasing you earlier when I said you should stay," I continued. "I really don't mind doing that first part alone, if you finish the second part."

"Sounds fair."

"I think I can get the first part done in about four hours. I've looked it over, and I think the second half will only take about three hours."

Erica groaned.

"What's the matter?"

"Three hours of work for you is six for me. I've got a tough day ahead of me tomorrow."

"It's a part of life. Just go on your date, relax, and worry about tomorrow, tomorrow."

"Easy for you to say. You won't have any work to do tomorrow."

I just looked at Erica for a moment. Was she kidding? Had she forgotten those children we had just discussed?

"Right, sorry. I guess I misspoke. What I meant to say was that you won't have any lab work tomorrow."

"But I have plenty for tonight. So if you're going to go, I wish you would go soon. I'll never get it all done if I don't get started."

"Aye, aye captain."

"Just go."

"That ought to do it," I declared loudly, attempting to punch a hole in the eerie silence that blanketed the lab. Unfortunately, it was more like a love pat. My modest little voice was no match for the powerful and monstrous night, with all of its potent sound-absorbing darkness.

It was my own fault that I was surrounded by silence; I could have brought along my own little cheer for this nighttime session in the lab. All I needed was an MP3 player, radio, maybe even the words to a song I could sing while I worked, but I did not have any of those things. It was not that I forgot—the truth was that I did not like adding my own sounds because I was just nervous enough to be alone in the building that I needed to be able to hear any and all noises. You know the ones, footsteps that stealthily snuck down the hall, the squeak of the lab door as someone crept in, the scratch at the window by an unseen watcher, the sound of…no, it was time to stop these imaginings. The goose bumps on my arms have grown to the size of cantaloupes, and I have a bad case of the shivers.

Why, oh why, did I watch all those scary movies in my teen years? What was my mother thinking to allow me to add all that horror to my mental arsenal? What was I thinking? My imagination has always been vivid and active, but now, after watching so many movies that filled me with terror, a lot of my imaginings were frightening.

It was just as well I had not brought along music, since it would have been the wrong kind of noise. The distant sound of happy voices or a vacuum off in the distance both reassured that other humans still existed and were nearby. The right kind of sounds made me feel safe.

Unfortunately, none of those happy sounds were audible on campus after ten p.m.. The dorms were all located on a different part of campus, and very few people had a legitimate reason to be in a deserted building in the middle of the night.

The janitors typically finished their work by ten and took their happy little vacuums with them. Security patrolled periodically, but their reassuring human presence was fleeting and sporadic. The noises that did not go away, the old-building noises that creaked and groaned and sighed—those noises in a way reassured me that humanity was nearby.

My nerves knotted at the thought, yet I adored that Denny Hall was such an old building. The oldest building on campus was the most appropriate location for the archaeology department. First occupied in 1895, this building had witnessed the momentous, the minor, and probably the mundane!

But I have digressed and allowed my thoughts to stray. Time to change my focus away from the past that surrounded me in this wonderful old building back to the past laid out in neat little piles on the table. My work was done except for a few minor details. As soon as they

187

were completed, I could pack up my belongings and head out.

I looked at my watch and chuckled. My prediction of four hours was right on target. Erica had left me to my work exactly three hours and fifty-four minutes ago.

I jotted down the final calculations, gathered up my papers, and cleaned up my area. Erica would pick up where I left off tomorrow as she completed her part of the project.

I was pleased that Erica had finally gotten the courage to start dating. Not that dating was so great, but without it, it was well nigh impossible to move to the next step and begin a family. That was where the real fun began.

I would take my crazy schedule—the late nights studying followed by early morning play sessions with the kids—over her dating woes any day. It had been a few years, but I could still recall the angst of not having a boyfriend, the anxiety of the first date, and the heartache of discovering that the guy I thought to be perfect was really a jerk.

No, give me married life any day.

At least...give me *my* married life. I'd heard the statistics, and I realized that not everyone was as fortunate as I was. My husband just happened to be my perfect match: Our values were based on the same moral system; we had similar goals and aspirations for our lives; our parenting styles could be better termed parenting style; and we appeared to be perfectly compatible in almost every way.

My husband was, and always would be, my best friend. Occasional squabble not withstanding, I had a deep-seated belief that I could always count on my husband to be there for me, just as I would always be there for him.

Everyone should have such a relationship with their spouse. It was what I wanted for Erica, who was rather fragile, and would be easily hurt if she put her trust in the wrong guy.

My good fortune was brought home to me when Tony and I started college. Nowhere could I find any other couples like us, since everyone I met was either single or had been remarried multiple times. Where were all the "normal" people with "normal" marriages? Tony and I had only been married ten years, yet everyone treated us as if we were a rare breed that was usually only seen in the wilds.

But once again, I have digressed. It was time to leave.

I'd finally gotten everything gathered up and my lab station ready for the next student when a humming noise startled me so much I jerked my hand back from the doorknob I had just grasped.

Shivers ran down my spine as I wondered what peculiar contraption had made such a noise. The strange, haunting drone could not have been made by a living creature—there was a definite mechanical quality to the sound.

189

I pulled my shoulders back, stood up straight, and flipped off the light switch. No haunting, outlandish, random noise was going to stop me from going home to my soft, lovely, comfortable bed.

I turned to look at the dark room behind me and was reassured by how normal everything looked in the pale moonlight leaching through the windows. I reached for the doorknob, and just as my hand touched it, I froze. There was the sound of footsteps just outside the lab door.

Not the footsteps of one person, many, many footsteps.

Who was in the building at this time of night?

I jerked my hand away from the knob as if it had suddenly become scalding hot. Fear overwhelmed me as I once again recalled my lonely state.

Tired or not, I'd rather wait a few minutes. Who knew what type of whackos were just outside.

Should I call security?

A movement caught my eye and I rushed over to the window. The street lights illuminated the area near the road to near-daylight standards, and I could see a group of ten to fifteen people moving swiftly down the street.

Two groups of this size would be too much of a coincidence, so this crowd must have just left the basement. Why had they been in Denny Hall?

I moved to the door to listen. Not a sound. No humming, no footsteps. Not even the sound of a little mouse scurrying around looking for a morsel left behind by a student and missed by the janitorial crew.

I had better get out of there while I had the chance. That group might have plans to return to Denny Hall for some nefarious purpose.

I inched the door open slowly, every muscle in my arm tensed to pull it closed quickly if need be. Relief washed over me as I realized that the hall was perfectly empty.

I grabbed my backpack and quietly exited the lab, gently closing the door and locking it behind me. As I tiptoed down the hall, I was surprised to notice that the janitor's closet was slightly ajar.

I had never before seen the janitor's closet ajar, so I immediately began to wonder if it was the work of the nefarious marauders who had just left the building. Could they have stolen something from the janitor's closet? Or done some damage? Or even worse, what if they left behind something dangerous, like a bomb, or drugs, or...or...who knows what dangerous item they might have left behind.

Darn! I'd never be able to sleep if I did not check. I had to take one little peek, just to make sure.

I gulped once and took a deep breath, disgusted that I did not really have a choice. Even as a little girl I had been compelled to check to make sure everyone and everything was safe. It was a curse. I could not walk away and ignore a potential problem.

Every time I had tried, I had spent hours upon hours waiting for something to happen.

I took a second deep breath and slowly let it out. I was ready for whatever I might find. I reached over, grabbed the handle, and jerked the door open.

Chapter 15

I MUST HAVE BUMPED MY head as I entered the janitor's closet, because my next conscious thought was of the cold, hard surface I was lying on and the visions of flying saucers and ice cream running through my head.

Come to think of it, the flying saucers and ice cream probably were not conscious thought—they were more likely part of a dream, a weird one.

Strange that I did not yet feel pain from the hit to my head. Something to look forward to, I guess.

I decided to keep my eyes closed for a few more seconds. The light filtering through my eyelids was blindingly bright. Or, to be perfectly

193

honest, I supposed it would be blinding if I were foolish enough to open my eyes and let it in full force.

I had no intention of doing anything so foolish quite yet, since chances were that bright lights plus a bumped head would equal a raging headache. I hated headaches. The longer I could put off the pain, the better.

Gingerly I reached up and carefully ran my hand over my head to assess the damage. Encouraged by the lack of wetness I conducted another search, this time for sore spots.

No bumps. No gashes. No bruises. No blood.

But I had lost consciousness; how could that be?

It was too late at night to try to unravel the Case of the Unconscious Woman. For now all I wanted to do was pick myself up, dust myself off, and head for the comforts of home.

Home, what a wonderful word. Just thinking the word brought visions of safety, comfort, family…a warm, soft. Just what I required for the glorious sleep that I desperately needed.

If I could just gather enough energy to open my eyes, rise from the floor, and drag myself to my car. Once I got to my car I could rest a few minutes.

Too many steps. It made me tired just to think about them. If I were not careful I'd end up finishing the night asleep in my car, or here on the floor of the janitor's closet, or maybe even curled up under a bush somewhere between Denny Hall and the parking lot—or, even worse, I might fall asleep....

The sound of voices, a lot of voices, interrupted my oh-so-unproductive train of thought. Instantly, adrenalin-laced fear banished the lethargy.

It must be the weirdos returning to complete whatever mischief they had planned. I needed to find a place to hide, and quick. I could not let them find me half-conscious on the floor.

Headache or no headache, it was time for action. My eyes flew open and I scanned the closet to look for the perfect place for quick concealment.

Only, it was not the closet I saw.

Blinking my eyes a few times did not change my view, so I tried a hard pinch to my arm. No success.

I stretched my arms out to my sides and brought them together as hard as I could, hoping the loud noise would shock me out of sleep. But it did no good.

Amazing, fantastic, extraordinary...horrible! Somehow, someway, I had been transported, probably while I was unconscious, out of that dinky, dirty little closet into a pristine, gigantic laboratory.

I did not understand. What possible reason would anyone have for moving me to a laboratory?

195

My spine become a Grand Prix racetrack, shivers racing up and down it so fast they must have broken the sound barrier.

Were those weirdos deranged scientists, scouring the campus for unlucky people they could kidnap to use in evil experiments? Was I their next unlucky victim? Had I fallen into the clutches—

A throat cleared just behind me. I was so startled I almost toppled off what I had thought was the floor, but turned out to be a table. I caught myself just in time to stop my face-first descent and swung around to confront the throat-clearer.

A man in a white lab coat stood there smiling at me. Just smiling.

What was wrong with the man? Why was he smiling? I had awoken to find myself in a strange place with no recollection of how I got here; I had almost fallen flat on my face; and my mouth felt like it was full of cotton. There was nothing to smile about.

"Well," the man exclaimed, "fancy seeing you here again! I am very surprised that you walked through that portal for a third time."

His manner was that of a jovial doctor trying to put his patient at ease. Did he think I was his patient?

Was I his patient?

"Oh, hello, um…doctor?"

His grin widened.

"Well...um...doctor, it's nice to meet you. I wonder if you could tell me where I am? And how I got here?"

"You don't remember me?"

"No, have we met before?"

He ignored my questions and asked one of his own. "Do you remember being here before?"

"No," I answered firmly. But inwardly I was trembling. Was this the doctor's subtle way of telling me that there was something wrong with my brain? Had I begun to forget things?

I gulped as the memory of those horrible days when I had forgotten the existence of my family flitted into my consciousness. I smiled a little as a vision of my daughters laughing and smiling filled my thoughts, and cringed as that vision was replaced by one of Becca handing me a camera to show me the evidence of my fashion-amnesia.

How horrible that I had contracted a disease that took chunks of my life away from me. I did not even remember that I was being treated for the disease!

"It's just as I thought," the doctor exclaimed rubbing his hands together like a scientist from an old movie, "you don't remember a thing about your previous visits here! The shielding was a success!"

This guy did not so much as chuckle, yet my mind had no difficulty adding the proverbial mad scientist laugh.

"A success!" I exclaimed, pushing aside all thoughts of mad scientists. "Whatever this shielding is, it is not working. I keep forgetting things."

"Yes, but—" the doctor began.

"I think we need to discuss changing my treatment," I said firmly, determined to have my say. I had no intention of allowing a doctor with mad scientist tendencies to make all the decisions. I would take control of my healthcare.

"What you need—" he began again, but I had more to say.

"Before we talk any further about what I might or might not need, I want my husband present. I would feel much more comfortable if he were a part of this."

"But—"

"Oh, I'm sure he was here for the original diagnosis. I'd never okay major treatment of any sort without letting him know about it."

"But—"

"But he should be here if we are going to discuss any changes."

"What are you blathering on about?"

Startled, I really looked at the doctor for the first time. He was calmly sitting on the table with his arms crossed casually in front of his chest, wearing an extremely irritating smile. It made me feel, somehow, as if I were being stupid.

"Blathering?" I asked in a hurt voice. Why would my doctor say something so rude to me? Something was going on here that I did not understand.

"Yes, blathering." He reached over and pulled out two chairs. "Why don't we sit down and get comfortable."

I took the offered chair and waited in trepidation. I had heard that if a doctor offered his patient a chair, it meant that he had bad news. Was he about to tell me that my prognosis was grim, and I should prepare to die? Or that I was crazy? Or worse, it might have fallen to the doctor to tell me that something had happened to my family.

A million possibilities ran through my head, each more horrible than the one before, until I happened to glance at the doctor.

He still sat there with that same smug smile, relaxed and at ease. Whatever he wanted to tell me, it was not bad news. No one could impart bad news with that happy, satisfied face.

I was still staring at his face, wondering how much I should worry, when the sound of his voice brought me back from my conjectures.

"Have you returned from wherever your worrying has taken you yet? I could tell you've been hither and yon, and I'd rather have you all here before I begin my explanation."

"I'm ready doctor," I stated solemnly, determined to give him my full attention. It was better to learn bad news firsthand, rather than speculate about all the horrible possibilities.

"First of all," the doctor said with a smile, "there is nothing for you to worry about. You aren't sick and your mind isn't slipping...as a matter of fact, the treatment you are getting has absolutely nothing to do with restoring your memory."

"I'm not sick? I'm not going to lose my memory?" I was so relieved I could almost hug the doctor.

"Not in the least," the doctor chuckled. "As a matter of fact, it is quite the opposite. We are working very hard to mask certain sections of your memories so that you won't remember them."

"What!" I yelled, jumping up out of my chair and slamming my hands down on the table. I no longer wanted to hug the man, I wanted to punch him. "I don't want anyone playing around with my memories! What kind of doctor are you?"

"Calm down, don't get so excited," the doctor said with a smirk. "There's no reason to worry. And by the way, I'm not a doctor, I'm a scientist."

"I can't believe it!" I yelled as my knees abruptly lost their ability to hold me upright and I plopped back down onto the chair.

"You can't believe—"

"I can't believe I was right in the first place," I continued more quietly, shaking my head in disbelief. "I can't believe I'm being held, against my will, in some sort of underground lab."

"You—"

"Don't try to bamboozle me! You're conducting illegal experiments on unwilling subjects! Admit it!"

"Not likely," the scientist said with a laugh. He seemed to be enjoying this. What kind of sick man was he?

"Not likely, not likely," I stammered, barely able to control the anger that had begun to bubble and brew in my veins. "What kind of answer is 'not likely'?"

"It is a simple answer. I'm a reputable scientist, and it is not likely that I would conduct those kinds of experiments."

I looked closely at the man noticed the earnestness in his expression. He truly believed that he was one of the good guys.

"Okay," I said, realizing I had to maintain my composure if I wanted the real scoop, "explain how I got here, why there are gaps in my memory, and what you have done to me!"

"No problem," came the unruffled reply.

Chapter 16

"GIRLS, IT'S TIME FOR BREAKFAST. Come to the table."

I had just cooked a scrumptious breakfast for my little munchkins, and I could not wait for them to taste it.

Cooking for a child was an adventure since it tended to be tricky. There was no logical rhyme or reason for a child's likes and dislikes—and they took eons to figure out. Then, just when you finally got it all figured out, her tastes would change.

Multiply that times three and cooking was not just an adventure, it was an expedition into the deepest wilds of the Amazon Rainforest.

Zoe, my youngest, ran into the room and immediately crawled under the table. Zoe never walked, but instead ran, skipped, or jumped. If there was any justice or sanity in the world, she had a mighty fine career as a track star ahead of her.

"Good morning, little one," I said with a smile. "Wouldn't you rather sit at the table, instead of under it?"

"Axshully, I like it here." My littlest child used the word "actually," or her version of it, in almost every sentence she spoke. How she had become so fascinated with it I had never been able to figure out. "I don't want ghosts to get me."

"Well actually," I responded with a smile, "I want you to sit at the table. I'll protect you from any ghosts that might come into my kitchen."

I held out my arms to her and she sprang from beneath the table straight into them. I gave my little jack-in-the-box a big hug, then I took advantage of her position in my arms to pick up the little cherub and plop her down in a chair. Her giggles were music to my ears.

From the hallway I could hear scurrying sounds, followed by soft whispers and repressed giggles—sure signs that my two oldest daughters were up to something. Before I had a chance to even wonder I found out what that something was.

"Whooooooooooo," a high-pitched voice moaned.

"Booooooooooo," another high-pitched voice groaned.

And there in the doorway where two sheet covered forms—my two oldest children.

Zoe stopped giggling and screamed.

I looked at her face in alarm, prepared to calm her fears and reprimand her sisters for scaring their little sister unnecessarily. But one look relieved my apprehension as I spotted that gleam of joy that meant she was simply caught up in play.

I had been a mother long enough to know that the best way to get children to do what you wanted when they were playing was to join in with their game of pretend.

"Oh, ghosts! I'm scared," I shrieked as I turned to Zoe and hugged her close. "What can we do, oh, what can we do?"

Zoe gave another little scream followed by a giggle. She was really enjoying this.

"Are you scared too, Zoe?"

Zoe's grin said she was not, but she nodded her head in the affirmative.

"But where are your sisters? Where can they be?"

"The ghosties ate them," the little munchkin answered with glee.

"Ate them! Oh no. What can we do?" I released Zoe from the hug and dramatically threw my head back with my hand on my forehead in the best old movie fashion.

"Get my sisters back!" Zoe demanded.

"You want me to get your sisters back?"

"Yes, Mommy," Zoe said with a nod, "and make ghosties leave!"

"You want the ghosties to leave? Do they scare you?"

"Axshully, no. I'm hungry."

"Got it! You want your breakfast and you are tired of this game."

"Yes, Mommy. I'm hungry."

"So be it," I said to the hungry cherub, "I'll work my ghost-removing, sister-bringing-back magic."

"Ghosts of the hallway, listen to my voice," I said sternly, turning to the apparitions in the hallway.

My daughters giggled, waved their arms more vigorously, and moaned and groaned more loudly.

"You are banished to the linen closet," I continued in a commanding voice, "bring back to me the children you have hidden."

"Not hidden, Mommy, eaten." Zoe was a precise child.

"Sorry," I said in a whisper to Zoe. Then I turned once again to the specters in the hallway and continued in my commanding ghost-removing voice, "spit out the children you have eaten and bring them back to me."

"Yuck," the biggest ghost said, but the other ghost just giggled.

"Even if they are all slimy with spit, bring back my children to me."

"That's just gross," the tallest ghost said. Both ghouls had now stopped their ghostly moaning and groaning and waving around of appendages. The tallest had assumed a hands-onhips stance, while the shorter one was doubled over with laughter.

"Be gone, ghosties! I command you! As master of this house, I command that you regurgitate my children so that they can eat their breakfast."

"Mom," Becca said as she pulled off the sheet, "you're gross."

"Hello Becca, it is good to see you back from the belly of the ghost," I said as I hugged my daughter.

"And Mom," Becca said pushing away, "you're not the master, Daddy is. You're the mistress!"

"Well what do you know—the girl thinks I can't be a master. Why does the master need to be your Daddy, Becky-girl?" I asked the ghost-turned-girl.

"Everyone knows the master is a man!" Becca said with a roll of her eyes to show exactly how silly I was being. "And you're not a man."

"Well, you've got me there. But who cares? What is so great about being the master, anyway?"

"Mom! The master is in charge!"

"In charge of what?"

"Everything."

"Everything?"

"Yes, Mom, everything."

"Who told you the master is in charge of everything?"

"No one told me, everybody knows that."

"I see. So the man is the master, and he is in charge of everything."

"Right."

"So what is the woman?"

"Like I said before, the woman is called the mistress," said my little font of wisdom.

"I think I understand. When you have a husband and a wife, the husband is the master, and the wife is the mistress. Right?"

"Yes, Mom, now you understand."

"So when there is a master and a mistress, who is in charge?"

"I told you already! The master, of course!"

"That's what I thought you'd say. I regret to inform you that you are wrong."

"Wrong?"

"Very wrong. I'll let you in on little secret. This secret has been passed down through the ages from mother to daughter, and I think it is time I passed it along to you girls."

Maddie, who had been listening intently to our exchange, immediately threw off her sheet and moved closer. Zoe hopped down from the chair and grabbed the bottom of my shirt, while Becca inched closer to listen intently.

There was nothing like a secret to get the full attention of my children!

I squatted down until I was eye-level with Maddie and leaned in, making our tight-knit circle even tighter. "You must promise never to reveal this secret to any of the uninitiated."

"Who are the un-sheeted?" Maddie asked seriously.

"All males are uninitiated."

"You mean letters, like from our mailbox?" Maddie's little face puckered up in confusion as she tried to picture telling a secret to a stack of letters.

"No, silly," Becca scoffed, "boys. Mom means boys are un-sheeted."

"Actually, the word is uninitiated," I gently corrected. "And it means, in this case, not part of the group. Men are male, and women are female. You girls will one day be women, so you have been initiated into the female group."

My little angels gravely nodded their heads.

"Okay, the secret that you must never reveal is that no matter what the men think, women are always in charge of their households."

"So women are really the masters?" Becca asked.

"No," I replied calmly, "women are really the mistresses."

"But I thought you said they are in charge?" Becca frowned as she posed her question. She disliked not having immediate understanding.

"Right, because being the mistress of a house *means* you are in charge."

"I don't understand, Mommy," Becca said, "if being the mistress means you are in charge, what does it mean if you are the master of a house, like Daddy?"

"It means that men are perfectly happy *thinking* they are in charge. And they will stay happy as long as we don't let them in on our secret."

All three girls stared at me, processing this new information.

"Mommy," Maddie questioned quietly, "are you telling us about a secret club?"

"Yes, my darling, very secret."

There was complete silence for a few minutes, until an exuberant smile broke out on Becca's face like the sun breaking through clouds on a summer's day.

"Mom," Becca asked excitedly, "can we be part of the club?"

"Oh sweetie, you already are!"

"Hooray," the three little girls cheered enthusiastically.

"Mommy," Zoe yelled, interrupting the merriment with more important matters, "my stomach is growly. Can we eat now?"

"Sure, baby. Have a seat at the table."

The girls eagerly took their places at the table, and I placed a plate in front of each of them. It was satisfying to see the gusto with which they dug into their food.

"Mommy, when is Daddy coming home?" Becca asked, putting her fork down next to her empty plate.

"Tonight twinkle-toes, why?"

"Well," my oldest said hesitantly, "I don't think he'll like your new way of cooking."

"New way of cooking?" I put down the pan I had been washing and turned to my daughter. What was she talking about? "I don't have a new way of cooking."

"Yes you do," Becca said firmly. "I like it, but Daddy won't like it."

"What won't your daddy like?" Was Becca starting a new pretend game, with me in the starring role?

"He won't like it that you put cinnamon and sugar in everything," came the reply.

"Sweetheart," I said with a smile. Children were so cute! "I don't put cinnamon and sugar in everything. This is french toast, it is supposed to have cinnamon and sugar."

"I know that, Mommy." Becca suddenly looked as if she was old and wise, and I was the young, unschooled child. "But you put cinnamon and sugar in our spaghetti last night. And the night before, you put it in our burritos."

"And for lunch yesterday we had peanut butter and cinnamon and sugar sandwiches. They were delicious!" Maddie chimed in, always the helpful one.

I slowly wiped my wet hands on a dish towel as I thought back over the last couple of days. Had I added cinnamon and sugar to everything?

Shock must have shown on my face, because Becca walked over to me and wrapped her little arms around me. "Are you okay, Mommy? Don't worry, we like the way you cook now!"

I smiled at my daughter and returned the hug. No reason to scare the children. I would just have to snap out of my most recent strangeness before Tony returned from his trip tonight.

What had I been thinking, to add cinnamon and sugar to every dish I prepared? What had I thought I was doing?

This must be related to my recent brain slippages. First I had forgotten my family, then I had forgotten how to dress, and now I had forgotten how to cook.

What was next? What else would I forget?

Was I going insane?

Chapter 17

"ERICA, DO YOU THINK YOU'LL be staying late tonight?"

As soon as the words were out of my mouth I wished I could swallow them back down. That one little sentence, that innocent little sentence, was an unintended recipe of manipulation. Very few people could resist the benevolence they felt when surrounded by the sweet smell of hope, especially when it was paired with the seemingly harmless flavor of joviality. But the secret ingredient—the subtle flavor of desperation—made this powerful concoction almost irresistible even to the most hardened.

But what had been said could not be unsaid. So I just pasted a mild smile on my face and awaited her response.

Our class had just ended for the day, and I had a ton of work to do before I could head home. It was a common enough occurrence for me, and I knew if I were alone I'd spend the next several hours concentrating on work with my forebrain while my backbrain listened for every unusual noise.

I've never actually found the word "backbrain" published anywhere, which I thought was a real shame. The term "forebrain" had been accepted, so why not backbrain? It only followed that if there was a front of something, there must be a back.

Besides, nothing else could so beautifully describe the location of that part of my mind that has activated every time I was alone in a creepy location, like the basement of Denny at night.

It made perfect sense. My eyes were located in front, so the front part of the brain could deal with what I could see. But what about all the things I could not see? What about everything left unattended behind me? That was where the backbrain came in.

The backbrain was in charge of alerting me to the sound of steps creeping up from behind, for raising the hairs on the back of my neck at the slightest hint of hot breath, for helping my muscles spring me to safety at the touch of an unseen hand.

The backbrain had one job, and one job only—to watch my back!

It was a great little system, but I would love to give it the night off. I had worked alone at night so much lately I was convinced my backbrain had earned a vacation—or at least a little down time.

The only sure way to give my backbrain time off was to have another living, breathing human in the lab with me. There was nothing like a friendly crowd, or at least a friend, to switch off the backbrain.

Several moments had gone by, during which Erica had continued with her task at hand as if she had not heard my question. I decided to repeat it. "Erica, do you plan to work here for a while tonight? Do you intend to stay late?"

"Oh, I will probably pull an all-nighter," Erica replied tartly, keeping her eyes focused intently on her work. "After all, I have nothing better to do with my time than spend it in this musty basement."

I looked at Erica sharply. Something was wrong. This girl was usually one of the nicest, most congenial people I knew.

Perhaps a little humor would lighten her mood.

"Musty," I joked, acting offended, "well, I'll have you know that we have the most efficient janitorial team in the country taking care of this building. Not only have they won awards for the last ten years from the Deft Eradicators of Refuse and Trash—more commonly know by the initials

DERT, which has an unfortunate pronunciation for people in the custodial world—but they have also gotten many accolades. They would be thoroughly offended if they heard you call their lovely, well-kept basement musty."

"Okay, maybe it's not musty," Erica said as she put down the potsherd she had been measuring.

"Glad you see it my way...I mean the janitorial team's way."

"But it *is* dark, dreary, and depressing." This came out not so much a statement as a moan. Erica gave up all pretense of work as she plopped down on one of the high stools and covered her face with her hands.

"Erica!" I cried in alarm. "What's the matter?"

Now I was worried. I had never seen spunky, chipper Erica depressed. Serious, yes, that was her usual state of being. But depressed?

"Wrong? What could be wrong? Just because I'm twenty-seven, no kids, no husband, no boyfriend, no male friends—sounds to me like my life is going along swimmingly!" The last words were rather wet, and accompanied by a pool of tears. I gathered up the papers that were in imminent danger of being submerged by the flood and moved them to safety. She would really drown in self-pity if I allowed this deluge to ruin days of work.

"Okay, what is going on? You were just fine at lunch time."

"Yeah, well, I'm a much better actor than you give me credit for. I didn't grow up the nerdy girl without learning a thing or two about hiding my hurt."

"Erica! You're feeling sorry for yourself! I've never seen you like this—you're usually so stoic. I thought you loved your life."

"Feeling sorry for myself? You bet I am. And why not? What is there about my life that I should be so happy about? Why *should* I love my life?" Anguish dripped from her words like poison. This was a side of Erica that I had not known existed.

"Hmmm, I think I see what you mean. There's absolutely nothing for you to be happy about."

"Nothing."

"Because really, loads of people get the chance to study archaeology here at the UW."

"I don't know if I'd say loads, exactly."

"And even though you are healthy and young, a lot of people are healthy and young."

"I don't not appreciate being healthy and young, its just that—"

"And I do feel sorry for you about your family. If you are feeling this way, it must mean that your family doesn't love or support you."

"Oh, no! My family is great. They—"

"Well then, it must be money problems. Would you like me to help you find a job? If you don't have enough money, it can cause extra stress. I'll be glad to help you redo your resume."

"That won't be necessary. I'm not having any money problems. I'm just lonely for—"

"Friends who share your interests? I understand. I'm an old married woman. What can we talk about? It seemed that we had things in common, but I understand if you don't want to be friends. Maybe it is time—"

"Wait! You're a great friend. I really enjoy our talks, hearing about your kids, being lab partners. But—"

"It's not enough. I understand. You cannot be truly happy unless you have a *real* friend. I guess I don't qualify."

"Of course you do! You're a great friend, there is none better."

"I'm a great friend?"

"The best!"

"And you don't have any money problems?"

"None whatsoever."

"And your family is supportive?"

"They are fantastic! They said they'll help me get a doctorate if that is what I want. And they are always sending me care packages, and calling, and—"

"If all these things are so great, what are you so unhappy about?"

"I don't have a boyfriend...," Erica began but stopped abruptly. She sat there staring at me for a few minutes, and then she pulled in a deep breath and slowly let it out. I could see the tension oozing out of her body as the reality of her good circumstances flooded in.

Erica probably would never realize her near escape from a big, messy, passionate meltdown that might have derailed her college career forever.

But me, I knew that people who were allowed full rein to feel sorry for themselves ran the risk of becoming so consumed by self-pity that all else in their lives got pushed aside. It was much better to intervene early, before they began to wallow in the gooey pit of despair. That pit was worse than quicksand, and was sure to suck a fragile person in deeper and deeper.

Luckily, this particular emotional tragedy seemed to be over for today. A little detective work was called for. If I found out what events triggered this explosive episode I could probably help prevent it from happening again.

"Spill," I gently commanded, "tell me what brought this on."

Not subtle enough. I could immediately see the tension flood again into Erica's body.

"What brought this on?" Erica screeched as she jumped off the stool, every muscle in her body poised and ready for a fight. Her voice mirrored the tension in her body and attained a pitch so high that I was sure that dogs for miles around would begin to howl in concert. "My life brought this on!"

My patience was beginning to run thin. We had just been through all this, and I did not have the time or the energy to go through it all again.

I did not mind commiserating with a friend, but I had no intention of promoting self-pity, which was what this looked like. Sure, this was probably based on something real, but Erica needed to understand that everyone in the world had troubles—no one led a perfect life. Anyone who said they did have a perfect life was lying.

Besides, who would like to lead a perfect life? What would be the fun of that? How could a person grow and learn without obstacles to overcome, mountains to scale, or oceans to swim?

I was of course speaking figuratively, not literally. I would never attempt to swim an ocean. I'd go by boat or plane—which illustrated my point exactly. Oceans and mountains were the very reasons that planes and boats were invented.

I needed to get to the bottom of this fast, before Erica could be sucked into the wretched quicksand of self-pity.

"Erica," I cajoled, "have you already forgotten what we just talked about? How fortunate you are to have your family, friends, and schooling as a part of your life?"

"I haven't forgotten...I've just decided that they aren't so wonderful."

"But why? Why would they be wonderful one minute, but not the next?"

"You don't understand."

"You're right, I don't. Explain it to me."

"I don't think I want to. You'll probably think I'm being silly."

"Try me."

"You won't understand."

"Give me a chance."

"You won't understand."

"Stop saying that and tell me already. Trust me to be your friend, and let me decide if I understand or not."

"Okay, okay. But try not to be too judgmental."

"I'll give it my best shot."

"It all began last year," Erica said despondently as she resumed her seat on the stool. Her demeanor showed no relief, only despair. "That's when my best childhood friend let me know that she is getting married. She wanted me to be her maid of honor."

"I don't get why that would upset you. You should be happy for your friend, and proud that she wants you to be her maid of honor."

"Oh, I am! I am very happy for her, and I was looking forward to the wedding. But then, about six months ago, another close friend emailed me that she had planned her wedding, and she wants me to be a maid of honor. I accepted. It will also be next month."

"Okay, so next month you'll be kind of busy. What's wrong with that?"

"I'm not done. Another close childhood friend had been dating the same guy for about five years. They finally set the date. And as you might be able to guess, it's for next month. She set it up that way just for me, because she wants me to be a maid of honor, and she knows I'll be in town for the other two weddings."

"I can see how three weddings in one month are a little tough. But it's still nothing to get so blue about."

"Let me finish. My little sister, she's three years younger than me, is also getting married. And the only time that his parents can get airplane tickets is, of course, next month. Since I'm her sister, she of course wants me to be her maid of honor."

"Your little sister is getting married? Aren't you excited about that?"

"I would have been if it weren't for my mother. She has decided to remarry for the fourth time. And guess when. Next month."

"Does she want you to be her maid of honor?"

"Fortunately, no. She just wants me to be there. Her wedding will be small and intimate."

"Doesn't that help, that you won't need to be your mom's maid of honor?"

"Yes, but not enough. I'll have the total of five weddings to go to—in two weeks. And not just go to, I'll be a part of the wedding parties. I'll be an integral part of ceremonies that will unite my three closest friends, my baby sister, and my mom to their soul mates."

"I still don't see why that's so depressing. Since your services as a maid of honor are so wanted, doesn't that mean that you are well loved?"

"Oh yeah, I'm well loved all right...by my female friends and family. But I want a guy of my own. I want to get married, find my own soul mate, have a family, and all that goofy stuff. I keep remembering that old saying, 'Always a bridesmaid never a bride.' Well, I want to be a bride."

"You'll get there. You're really not as old as you think you are."

"Oh, and how old were you when you got married?"

"What does that have to do with anything?"

"Come on, tell me, how old were you?"

"Okay, so I was twenty-three. But in this day, age, and geographic location, that is rather young. And I just got lucky that I found my husband so early."

"Lucky—right. So how do I get a little of that luck?"

"If I knew, I would tell you."

"Do you have any advice? Something that would help bring that luck alone?"

"Well, there is one thing..."

"What?"

"I don't know if it will work for you."

"What is it?'

"Some say it is just an old wives' tale."

"Tell me!"

"Well, they say that if you want to find your true love, place a piece of wedding cake under your pillow at night. You are sure to dream of your future husband."

"You think I should try it?"

"You'll sure have plenty of chances next month. I wouldn't hurt."

"I'll give it a try."

"Great. Only..."

"Only what?"

"Be careful."

"Careful of what?"

"Careful of dreaming of five different guys! I'd stop as soon as my mind grabbed hold of the first one. You don't want to complicate matters."

"Will do."

"So are we past the danger zone? Are you ready to buckle down and get our work done?"

"As ready as I'll ever be."

"Great, because this project is due Friday, and we won't have many more chances to work late."

※　※　※

"Vanessa, do you hear that?" Erica whispered in my ear, startling me so that I jerked sideways. As my stool began to tilt dangerously I struggled to unwrap at least one of my feet from its legs. I detangled one foot just in time to slow my descent, but not quick enough to avoid disaster entirely. My only hope was to use my arms to regain control, but my flailing arms only succeeded in clipping Erica on the nose as I crashed to the floor.

"Erica!" I exclaimed as I picked myself up and brushed a thick layer of dust from my pants. I was beginning to rethink my kind words about the custodial staff. The floor was quite dirty. If I had any say in the matter, at least one of those DERT awards would be rescinded.

"Shhh," Erica shushed softly, "don't shout. I asked you if you heard that noise."

"What noise?" I questioned grumpily. But as I watched Erica rub the end of her nose where I'd clipped it, I began to feel a little less grumpy. That red bump right on the tip was an excellent reward for her concentration-breaking stunt. She had worked with me often enough to know that when conditions were just right, like tonight, an eighteen-wheeler could drive up beside me and I would not notice. What had she been thinking to sneak up on me like that?

"That humming noise…do you hear it?"

I rolled my eyes and sighed. What was getting into Erica lately? Where had my level-headed friend disappeared to, and who was this stranger who had taken her place? Had her desire for a husband and family unbalanced her mind? Was she slipping into—

"I'm not crazy," Erica said quietly, as if she had read my mind. Then she looked me straight in the eyes and placed her hand on my arm, "Just listen."

Erica's eyes pleaded for me to listen as her hand shook with tension. She was either seriously worried about something, or her current wedding stresses had unhinged her much more than I had previously thought. Five weddings in two weeks probably were enough to stress the best and most grounded of us.

But maybe there was a simple way I could help Erica resolve her stressed out state. At home, when my children were upset, I have found that a little extra attention often calmed their fears.

I could be a good friend to Erica and give her that one-on-one attention she craved. She was far from her family, so it had probably been months since she had had another human's undivided attention. She needed to reconnect with humanity and feel that she was indeed an important person in someone's world.

It certainly would not hurt me to push aside the project for a few minutes and play along. After Erica's fears were calmed, and she regained her emotional equilibrium, we could get back to work.

I tilted my head to one side and listened— determined to put on a good show so that I could reassure Erica that her fears were unfounded. I was certain that the noise she had mentioned was merely the highway in the distance, or wind rustling the bushes outside the window. Erica deserved to see that her fears were getting the attention they warranted.

So there I was, posed in the stereotypical listening stance, straining to hear wind whistling through leaves or the drone of tires on asphalt. I heard neither. Instead, the sound that reached my ears was an odd whirling whine that came not from outside, but from within the building.

"Do you hear it? Do you hear the sound?"

"Yes. Yes, I do." The surprise must have shown in my voice, because Erica abruptly sat back and raised one eyebrow.

"You didn't believe me, did you?" I could hear the hurt in her voice.

"It's not that I didn't believe you," I reassured her calmly, "I just didn't hear it before."

I continued to listen to the puzzling noise for a few more minutes as Erica stared at me.

"Fair enough," she finally said with a smile and a nod, obviously deciding to accept my answer.

I nodded in return. I was relieved that a crisis had been averted, but even more, I was happy that Erica reassumed her place in the world as my mild-mannered, level-headed friend.

"I've never heard that noise during the day," she continued. "You've worked here late at night more than I have; have you ever heard it before?"

"I...I'm not sure." I answered slowly. I had no memory of the noise, yet it seemed strangely familiar. Most familiar of all was the tingly sensation circulating through my body. I felt like a giant tuning fork—alive with the vibrations electrifying the air.

"What do you mean, you're not sure?" Erica asked, irritated by my lack of clear-cut answer.

Erica was deep down a very black-or-white type of person who did not like dealing with gray areas or unknowns. I had never understood why she had chosen to study archaeology, with all of its quasi-unsolvable mysteries and shadow answers.

"Well," I said hesitantly, "I don't remember hearing that sound before, but I have a feeling that it is familiar, like a distant memory that I can't quite grasp."

"Maybe," Erica said with all appearance of seriousness, "you have been hypnotized to immediately forget any random noises you hear while you are working. And you have heard the humming before, but only while working. So of course, your conscious mind discarded the memory, while your subconscious heard it and retained the memory."

"Are you taking a psychology class this quarter by chance?" I asked.

"You'd better believe it! It will fulfill some of the requirements I need outside my major."

"Great," I continued in an effort to lighten the mood, "I wish you would have warned me sooner. I would have picked another lab partner. And are you now going to conduct further analyses?"

"Not on you," Erica said as a mischievous smile broke out on her face, "there is no need since I already know you're crazy—in your own special way. Why else would you be here, in the basement of a creepy old building when you could be sleeping peacefully in your own bed?"

"Oh no! It...it...it can't be true," I stuttered, shaking my head in denial.

"What can't be true?" Erica's smile slipped as her brow furrowed.

"I won't believe it! I won't, I won't."

"What? What won't you believe?"

"No, no, no! It is too, too horrible!"

"What is too horrible?"

"I didn't want to believe it was true, I hoped it wasn't true, but I must accept it—"

"Accept what? Tell me, what must you accept?"

"I must accept the horrible truth."

"What is the horrible truth?"

"That...that...that you are crazy!"

"Me, crazy? What are you talking about?"

"Well...," I began in a whisper, but then I dropped my head. "No, I can't. I can't tell you."

"What? What can't you tell me?" Erica's face now looked so serious I knew she had forgotten that she had really started this whole thing.

"No, I can't do it. It will devastate you." The drama was building very nicely, very nicely indeed.

"I'm strong—you can tell me what I've done that makes you think I'm crazy."

"Are you sure you can take it? Are you positive you want to know?"

"I...," Erica gulped, "I'm sure. Tell me."

"Okay, if you're sure...," I bent close and whispered the next part directly into her ear. "You're here."

"What?" Erica's face showed total confusion.

"Well," I continued in a normal voice, "you claimed that I was crazy because I was working here late at night. But you are also here. Therefore, since a late-night presence in the archaeology lab is proof of mental instability, you must also have lost all your marbles."

I watched as comprehension dawned and Erica's smile returned.

"Gotcha!" I said, returning her smile. "You really need to work on your gullibility. You fall for all my jokes entirely too easily."

"I'll work on it. But you know, I think your logic is sound."

"What do you mean, my logic is sound?"

"I think that our presence here late at night is proof that we are both certifiable. No doubt about it."

"And you know this because of your class?"

"Oh no, we won't get into that stuff for another few weeks."

"So you know..."

"I know because my common sense tells me that no sane person would waste hours and hours staring at broken pieces of pottery."

I looked hard at Erica and could immediately see that she was at least partly serious—understandable, after so many hours of work.

"I think your common sense is absolutely correct. We must be nuts," I said with a nod.

"But all kidding aside," Erica continued, "I want to talk about that humming noise. What could make that kind of noise in a building like this?"

"Who knows? Maybe," I said as I straightened my papers a bit, "maybe there is a secret laboratory hidden beneath this building, and top secret experiments are being conducted there late at night."

"Come on, I said kidding aside! That sounds like a plot from an old movie."

"Or several."

"Several?"

"Oh, yes. That plot has been used in loads of old movies. And in a few newer ones too."

"When," Erica asked in apparent shock, "do you have time to watch old movies?"

"I'll admit that I haven't watched any recently. But when the girls were babies, they all seemed to go through a phase where they had their days and nights confused. After a few hours of walking them I would get bored and turn the TV on with the sound low. Some channels play old movies late at night."

"Makes sense," Erica nodded with understanding, "so why haven't you watched lately?"

"None of my kids are that age now. They all sleep through the night just like the little angels they are. But I've have enough late nights here at the lab that I'm not going to pass up a single opportunity for sleep. The old movies will just have to wait until my life becomes a little less cluttered."

"Can't say that I blame you."

"Hey, wait—listen."

"Listen to what?"

"The humming."

"I don't hear the humming."

"That's what I mean. It stopped. Those mad scientists must be done with those oh-so-secret experiments they were conducting in the middle of the night in the secret laboratory lair."

"Right."

"About how much longer," I said as I tried to stifle a yawn, "do you think you need to work?"

"You know, I think—" Erica began, but had to pause for a yawn of her own. "Sorry. I think I'm at a point I can easily finish tomorrow. Do you want to call it a night?"

"That is absolutely the best plan I've heard in eons. But let's just be careful as we leave that we don't run into any mad scientists roaming the halls."

"Right you are. We'll use extreme caution."

What fun it was to have someone to joke with in the wee hours of the night. It certainly lightened the mood.

I gathered all my papers and inserted them into my backpack, while Erica gathered her papers and put them in her briefcase. I had never been able to understand why she chose a briefcase over a backpack, but I was sure she had her reasons.

"Are you ready?" I asked as I finished straightening my work station. I looked over and saw that Erica's station was already all neat and tidy.

"Let's go!" Erica said energetically.

I looked at her with disgust. Where had she gotten enough energy to even *pretend* that much exuberance at one a.m.?

Frankly, I really did not care. I simply wanted to go home and get some sleep. If Erica wanted to be full of vim and vigor in the middle of the night, that was her business. My business was to go home and recharge for the next day.

I noticed Erica standing by the open door with her hand on the light switch, so I quickly shoved the remainder of my papers into my backpack. That suspicious energy might mean that Erica was planning retribution, and I was afraid her plan was to enjoy the slapstick humor of me stumbling across the darkened room while she waited safely by the door.

Thankfully, I had credited Erica with cruel thoughts that she did not have, because the light stayed on until I was safely across the room. Or perhaps her lack of cruelty was intended as a model for me?

Erica was becoming curiously wily. Maybe I should take one of those psychology classes. I might learn a thing or two.

"Do you have your keys?" Erica asked as she dug through her purse, "I left the set that has the lab key on it at home."

"No problem," I answered. "I'm here so often I always have the lab keys with me. I'll lock up."

I struggled to secure the door, aggravated to find that quite a few jiggles were required before I could get it to lock.

"This darn lock," I said in frustration as I tried and failed to remove it from the lock, "does your key stick like mine?"

"No," Erica shook her head, "or at least not the last time I tried it. Maybe your key is bent."

I finally managed to wiggle the key out of the lock and held it up to the light. Erica was right. The key was bent. No wonder I had had so much trouble with it. I would have to find time in my schedule tomorrow to go to the archaeology office and trade this crooked one for a new one.

I swung around to show the twisted key to Erica, and my upraised hand hit the can of super-duper caffeine drink that she had just swigged. The can flew from her hand and hit the wall, causing the dark liquid to pour down the wall, over the floor, and splash onto Erica's head.

"I'm so sorry, Erica!"

"Don't worry." Erica said as she tried to flick drops of liquid energy from her hair. "It's my fault for not getting out of the way of your thrashing hands fast enough."

"Thanks for accepting my apology so graciously, and for pointing out my clumsiness."

"No problem, any time," came the reply.

"Oh, what a mess," I said disgustedly as I looked around the hallway. "Now I'll have to go through the whole key routine again so we can get some paper towels from the lab to clean it up."

"You could spend the next twenty minutes doing battle with your bent key," Erica said, "or we could just get the paper towels from the janitor's closet over there."

"We can't get into the janitor's closet, it's always kept locked."

"Well, it's unlocked now."

"Are you sure?"

"I'm positive—just look, it's open. And if you want my vote, we'll fast track our cleanup by getting the paper towels the quick and easy way."

I looked toward the janitor's closet, and was surprised to see that the door was indeed ajar just a bit.

As I looked at that little crack between the door frame and the door, a little voice in my head began to whine that this door spelled trouble. It moaned and groaned that if I approached it, I would be making a very bad mistake.

I ignored the irritating little voice. It was obviously the result of viewing too many late night old movies with sinister plots.

Chapter 18

"WHERE ARE WE?" ERICA WHISPERED. Her eyes were gleaming with excitement and not a trace of fear showed in their blue depths.

"The janitor's closet?"

"This is not like any janitor's closet I've ever seen! Where do you really think we are?"

"I'm not sure, but it looks like a laboratory of some sort."

"That's what I thought too." Erica said, nodding her head.

Then with what I supposed was an effort at drama, her voice deepened and she began to speak like Vincent Price, the king of scary. "We now find ourselves in a secret, underground laboratory where mad scientists conduct nefarious experiments late at night. We have unfortunately wandered into their trap and will become the next unwilling subjects of those horrible experiments."

"Ha…ha…ha," I said, in the most sarcastic voice I could manage. In reality, fear had set my insides trembling like a bowl of lemon-flavored Jell-O traveling at sixty miles per hour on a wooden rollercoaster ride, for I thought there was more than just a bit of truth to Erica's little scenario. From what I could see, we *had* most likely fallen into the clutches of an underground group—one with very few scruples.

"What sort of experiment do you think they intend to conduct?"

I turned to glance at Erica. Her face was glowing with excitement, and she looked exactly like a child who had just been given her first bicycle—and a puppy.

"Erica," I asked cautiously, "are you feeling okay?"

"All right," Erica responded eagerly, "I feel better than just okay. I feel fantastic, wonderful, stupendous—I feel better than I ever felt in my entire life!"

"Erica," I asked as I grabbed her arm, "what's going on? What is wrong with you?"

"Nothing is wrong, everything is right!"

"But you are acting so strange. You aren't acting like *you*!"

"Look, I don't know about not acting like me, and I don't know what's going on. All I know is that I feel more alive than I ever have in my whole life. Don't you feel it? Take a deep breath. It's so vibrant, like...like...like I'm breathing in vitamins—or life. Like every breath is making me healthier and healthier, more and more alive. Don't you feel it?"

As I watched my friend, I could see her transforming right before my eyes: her cheeks became rosier, her eyes brighter, and her back straighter. But the most important change was not in her physical appearance so much as her mental. A certain look that had always lurked in the back of Erica's eyes, a look that let me know that Erica was not comfortable in her own skin, that she somehow felt she was not as good as everyone else—that look was gone.

Sitting beside me was my lab partner, but not quite the same lab partner I had grown to know. I did not know how it had happened, but my overly serious, confidence-lacking, somewhat dull lab partner had been replaced by a new and improved version.

It was as if the simple act of walking through the closet door moments earlier had caused Erica to grow up, throw off all of her self-doubt, and become a confident and happy young woman. The transformation was stunning!

I took a deep breath, eager to taste the wonderful elixir that could cause such an instantaneous makeover. The air certainly did not smell like the basement of Denny Hall; I could smell no dust or mustiness. Instead there was a freshness reminiscent of forests, and ocean breezes, and sunshine.

Disappointed, I decided Erica's imagination had played tricks on her. All I was breathing was plain old, perfectly normal air. This lab simply had a better ventilation system than most.

"Look at this place, it is amazing!" Erica sighed, her voice full of wonderment. I pulled my attention away from the captivating mysteries of circulating air back to the activity around us.

As we watched, white-coated minions scurried about—looking surprisingly like those little silver balls in a pinball machine. There was so much activity, so much hurrying, that I began to wonder if anyone had even noticed our presence. Maybe our best bet would be to find a way to sneak out, as if we had never entered this secret lair of frantic motion.

Unfortunately, my thought came too late. At the exact moment the brilliant idea of escape began to shine in my head, a dazzling light drew my attention to the entrance of two men. It was immediately evident who they were, or at least what they were.

As often happens when bosses enter a room, there was a subtle but instantaneous shift in the actions of the workers. The subordinates no longer scurried around willy-nilly like pin balls; instead, they each took a quick look at management and adjusted their movements to more purposeful and intelligent routes—like robots in a well-choreographed factory.

Management casually strolled in our direction, heads together deep in conversation. So intent were they with their discussion, so assured of their way, that they never once looked up to check their path was clear of obstacles. Obstacles like Erica, or me. I again wondered if anyone knew of our existence, since management was on a direct collision course. If they continued as they were going, Erica and I needed to find a new place to sit, or brace for impact.

The men continued their seemingly oblivious promenade until they were a mere three feet away. Just as I was about to jump up rather than be bowled over the men stopped.

I was so shocked I almost fell off my chair when the elder of the two looked me right in the eyes, smiled wryly, and said, "Well hello, Vanessa. I can't sincerely say that I'm pleased to see you again. Especially since this time you chose to bring along a friend."

I gulped and stared at the man, willing my brain to recall where and when I had met him before. But it was no good—I could find no memory of his face filed away in my brain.

Was this another sign of memory loss?

Or worse, had I entered the Twilight Zone?

No matter. I knew my best course was to put aside any doubts and show the best manners I possibly could. Twilight Zone, memory loss, or mad scientist, good manners and diplomacy would probably bring about the best response.

"It is very nice to meet you," I said with as much confidence as I could muster. "I'm afraid that even though you have been informed of my name, I don't yet know yours. And in case no one has told you, this is my friend Erica. She and I work together on many projects..."

I had turned to indicate Erica during this artfully diplomatic introduction, but my words stopped flowing as my jaw dropped open in shock. Never, in the three years I had known her, had I ever seen Erica look at a man as she was looking at this one. And by this one I meant the younger man, not the older one.

I could not comprehend why she was staring at the man with such rapt attention. He was in every way I could see just an average man—average height, average weight, average looks—nothing special to write home about.

It was obvious Erica saw something that I did not. She was gazing into his eyes as if she were deeply, desperately, unconditionally in love.

Even more amazing was that the man was gazing back with the same love-sick expression on his face.

I was perplexed, flabbergasted, and bewildered. I had never seen two people go ga-ga for each other so quickly or completely. Not only did they not know each other's names, neither had spoken so much as a word since coming into the other's presence! Would the goofy expressions on their faces change to disgust if one of them had an accent the other could not tolerate? Would the blossoming love wilt if they found they had nothing in common?

On the bright side, at least we did not need to worry about being experimented on—unless Erica was unfortunate enough to fall in love at first sight with a married man.

At that thought I sighed in resignation. It was up to me to protect my oh-so-naive friend. If this guy was married, every minute Erica stayed in the state of infatuation would only make her heartbreak more painful. I needed to clarify the situation, and I needed to do it fast.

"Hey, you," I called to the love-struck young man, "I want to talk to you a minute."

Based on the effect my voice had it appeared that love had made the man deaf. "Excuse me," I continued more loudly, waving my hands in the air. "I'm talking to you. Hey, over here, hey you…with the goofy face."

With supreme effort the man finally managed to pull his gaze away from Erica and turned his startled face in my direction.

Now that he was no longer gazing soulfully at Erica I could see that he did have rather nice eyes. Not as nice as my husband's stunning, mysterious brown pools of intensity, but good enough that a newbie like Erica could be easily transfixed.

"I want to know," I asked firmly, "what are your intentions toward my friend?"

"My...my...my what?" The poor man looked thoroughly confused. "What do you mean by my intentions?"

"Well," I explained calmly, "you are staring at my friend hungrily, as if she was an eight course meal and you hadn't eaten in a week."

"I am very sorry," the man said contritely, closing his eyes and taking a deep breath to regain his composure. "I apologize for my rude behavior. It's just that as soon as I saw your friend I felt this connection..." He glanced sideways at the older man, embarrassment obvious on his face.

"Okay, you felt a connection." I said tersely, determined to protect the interests of my friend. "Are you free to follow up on that feeling?"

"I don't think I understand what you are asking." The man's tone was now haughty and his face red, a sure sign that he was in extreme emotional discomfort.

"I'm asking you if you are married." I kept my tone firm but level. I wanted answers, not aggression. "I want to know if your interest in my friend is honest. If—"

"Of course my interest is honest," he burst out, not letting me finish my sentence. And then he hung his head shyly, "I think she is wonderful."

"Great, we are in agreement that my friend is a wonderful human being. But you still haven't answered my main question. Are you married?"

"No," he answered decisively, "I'm not married."

"Now that we've got that cleared up," I said, turning again to the older man, "I wonder if you could tell my friend and me exactly where we are. I'm very surprised to find that a lab of this size—one that we've never heard of—exists right under our noses. What department does this lab belong to?"

"Excellent," was the man's response.

I looked from the older man to the younger, astounded by the huge smiles that had exploded onto their faces. What had I said to cause such euphoria?

"I had wondered," the younger man said gleefully to the older man, nodding his head in evident satisfaction.

"What had you wondered?" This conversation was not going quite how I had planned.

"Well, we've been through this so many times I'd wondered if the shielding had been successful or not. But your questions assure me that it was a success. You don't remember your previous trips here at all, do you?"

I gulped, concerned to hear the term "previous trips" spoken so casually. Reluctantly, I shook my head no.

Erica, who had most likely been scampering about tossing flowers into the air in an imaginary wonderland, gave herself a little shake and turned a speculative glare in my direction. "You've been here before? You've met these people, all of them, before?"

Erica's voice did not hold a tinge of jealousy, it dripped with it.

What luck! Here I was, present at the birth of a budding romance between my closest female friend and her soul mate. But instead of being able to share my friend's joy, jealousy had reared its ugly head and wedged its disgusting self smack-dab in the middle of our friendship. All because I had met the guy of her dreams before she had.

My hope was that the jealousy would abate as soon as I had explained how truly insignificant the meeting had been to me. After all, I had not even remembered it.

* * *

"Thank you for explaining it all to me...again." I had just had a tour of the lab, a light snack, and an in-depth explanation of how I got here, where here was—and when. Erica had been thoroughly fascinated with the explanation but had, for reasons known only to herself, wanted to see the ventilation system. She was now being escorted around the building by the young man, both of them looking at the other as little as possible.

I still could not believe that this was my fourth trip to this laboratory, or that these people had a way to erase memories. Most strange of all was that this was the future; so far into the future that there was no possibility my non-time-traveling self could be alive.

Was this real, or had I fallen into a science fiction movie?

"No problem," Doc replied. "Having to explain again reassures me that the shielding worked. Even if there were a few glitches."

Doc was the older man I had correctly tagged as management, and he was indeed the boss. Doc was not really his name, or even a name used by anyone else. No one had used any names whatsoever in my presence.

I had asked Doc to tell me his name since I was tired of saying "hey you" all the time, but he had refused, claiming that if I managed to remember it later it could prove dangerous. I decided the name "Doc" fit him as well as any other. I hoped he did not mind.

"Doc," I asked, "how are you going to stop these trips I keep making to the future? Erasing my memory is all well and good, but evidently it doesn't stop me from returning."

"Just to be clear, I should explain that we don't actually erase your memory. The memories all stay in place. We only cover them so that your mind can't find them."

"Fine. Glad to know it. But what do you plan?"

"I've spoken to our best scientists, and we've come up with a solution that I think will work."

"Which is...?"

"We're going to have to try something a little different this time. After I shield you, I'll have you placed in a state of hypnosis, and you will be given very specific suggestions."

"Hypnosis?"

"It's the best way. But don't worry, I will send an operative to make sure you get home safely. He won't release you from the hypnotic state until you're safely on your doorstep. We'll make sure you don't remember that part. After a few hours of sleep, you should be normal, fully refreshed, but with no memory of your trip."

"How will it be different?"

"The suggestion we plan will give you a very strong aversion to the portal."

"An aversion to the portal?"

"Yes. It is a beautiful plan. You won't remember your trip here, and we'll never have to worry about you wandering back. Just the thought of going through the portal into our lab will make you feel ill. We will implant the picture of the portal into your brain with so much aversion that you will not be able to make yourself open the portal to step through."

"You're sure this will work?"

"Have no fear, you won't be back. It's been nice meeting you…I hope you have a nice life."

"Wait a minute! If this is the future, shouldn't you know if I'll have a nice life or not?"

"Of course I know! I just can't tell you, or give you any clues. Besides, it is only an expression. Much like have a good day, but it covers a longer period of time. Much longer."

Chapter 19

"SWEETHEART, IT'S TIME TO WAKE up," whispered a voice in my ear. It was Tony's voice, so it must have been his hand that gave my shoulder a quick little shake.

I rolled over and gazed at my husband. He had the biggest, deepest, most beautiful brown eyes in the world. Eyes that were worth waking up for, eyes that made me determined to shake off the last vestiges of sleep and return to the waking world. Their gorgeous, intense depths reached out, grabbed my soul and hugged it tight; while their softness blanketed my heart with cuddly warmth. Eyes with such intense softness—combined with untold depths—was enough to make a girl sigh.

My husband had many great qualities. I loved that he was a man of integrity—if he made a promise, he would do everything in his power to fulfill that promise. He was a man of ethics and could be trusted to do the right thing. I would trust him with my life in a heartbeat. I also loved that he was smart, witty, and kind.

I was supremely fortunate that not only did our values match—surprising since we came from very different backgrounds—but so did our sense of humor. I have never had to worry that he would think my silly little jokes too immature. I never had to watch what I said for fear my comments would be misunderstood.

We laughed at the same jokes, were saddened by the same injustices, and felt free to discuss the few times we disagreed. We matched so perfectly that he was not only my husband, but he was my best friend.

But good conversation, a great sense of humor, and shared values were not enough for a good marriage. Not nearly enough!

It took great eyes.

I'd have to make it a personal policy to gaze deeply into my sweetheart's eyes, oh…every month or so, or maybe daily. I could recapture that wonderful, glorious feeling of souls connecting. I could remind myself why I fell in love with this man in the first place. His eyes are fantastic! Deep, dark eyes, like giant pools of sweet, warm, creamy chocolate. Chocolate so smooth a person could swim in it. Chocolate…

"Darling," my husband whispered as he gently brushed his fingers across my cheek, "don't go back to sleep again. Aren't you ready to wake up yet?"

His touch jerked me back from the abyss of chocolate heaven. I had not even been aware that I had been drifting off to sleep.

"Let me help you sit up. That will help you wake up," Tony mumbled. He reached over, grasped my arms, and tenderly pulled until I was in a sitting position. He was being extremely gentle and kind, a huge improvement over how the kids woke me.

I tried to be up before my children every morning, but once a week or so I tended to oversleep. On those days my little munchkins had a routine from which they rarely varied.

First they would sneak as quietly as mice into my room and climb up onto the footboard. Then with perfect synchronization, so perfect it could only be achieved by beings that sprang from the same gene pool, they would jump. And jump and jump and jump.

My bed would cease to be a place of rest and repose, and would instantly transform into a trampoline. It did not matter how often or how loudly I complained of blossoming bruises, the persistent little devils would laugh and giggle and out-jump my complaints. It usually only took about two minutes before I gave up and climbed out of bed, clearing the way for the entire bed to be used as a trampoline.

The girls would only jump on the bed for another minute, so I suppose the bed-as-trampoline-game was only a secondary target. The real goal was me.

I stretched my arms over my head and yawned. Tony was right. Based on the sunlight streaming through the window, it was past my normal time to rise and start the day. Ribbons of light filtered through the curtains to create beautiful patterns on the wall, spotlighting fragments of dust that danced and frolicked in the sun's rays. Even the tiniest of objects was trying to tell me I needed to get up and enjoy the wondrous world in which I lived.

"You know, Tony," I said with another yawn, "I feel great. I think that was the best night's sleep I have had in years! I feel like I've slept for days."

"Well, you almost have. You slept a whole day through. You came home from the lab the night before last so tired you couldn't even talk. You went right to sleep, and no matter how noisy the girls were, you slept right through it. I was beginning to worry."

I sat up straighter and shifted around to get a better look at my husband. Was this a joke?

"I slept a whole day?" Even I could hear the disbelief in my voice.

"An entire day," Tony replied seriously. He reached over and gingerly patted my hand.

If I had slept through an entire day it was little wonder that he was handling me with kid gloves. I get tired occasionally just like everyone else, but I can usually hang in there. Sleeping for an entire day was bizarre.

"So if I've been asleep so long, what did you do with the girls?"

"I took care of them, of course. Like any good father would. I do have a few parenting skills, you know."

"But what about your schedule? Did you have to miss work or your classes?"

"Luckily I wasn't scheduled for a flight, so I just skipped my classes and contacted my professors to get what I missed. It was no problem."

"Well, what about dinner last night? And breakfast...and lunch...and snacks? What did you feed the girls?"

"Relax. I pour a delicious bowl of cereal, make a mean peanut butter and jelly sandwich, and I found directions right on the back of the box that told me how to cook macaroni and cheese. I even cooked some peas, so the girls could have a well-rounded meal."

I sat there thinking. Had I really been that tired? What had made me sleep so long? Was it going to happen again?

"Are you sick?" Tony asked quietly, worry clouding his face.

I wiggled my back around, stretched my neck, and lifted my arms over my head. "I don't feel like I'm sick. It could be normal tiredness. I have been working late for quite a few weeks now."

"But this is not the first time you've put in long hours, and you've never slept through the day like this before."

"True."

"Not even after the birth of any of the girls. It's not normal for you to sleep this long."

"I don't think it's normal for anyone," I said with a sigh. "But I'm awake now and ready to start the day. Are the girls up yet?"

"Are you kidding? They have been up for hours," he said quietly. "They are being particularly mice-like because they think you are sick."

"What time is it?"

"It's just about eleven o'clock. The girls are afraid you're going to sleep another day away. Maddie has gotten out the Sleeping Beauty book and has been reading it over and over. Then she comes in and looks at you with a worried expression on her little face—"

"I've slept a full day through, and now it's eleven?"

"Eleven. So do you think you were just behind in your sleep...," Tony's tone and expression were equally serious, "or do I need to take you to the doctor because you have some rare sleeping sickness?"

I never have been very good at maintaining a proper serious attitude for any length of time, and the "rare sleeping sickness" question combined with the thought of my daughter and her Sleeping Beauty book jolted me right out of the somber mood. I let myself fall back on the pillow, closed my eyes and put my hand up to my forehead.

Tony immediately grabbed my shoulders, concern evident in his every movement. "Are you okay?" he asked worriedly.

"I am just so tired. I think I need...."

"What? What do you need?"

"I think I need you to...."

"What darling, what do you need me to do? Tell me!"

"I need...," I paused for a moment to deepen the drama, opened one eye so I could watch the effect of my words, and then continued, "I need my Prince to kiss his Sleeping Beauty!"

I burst out laughing at the blank expression on my husband's face. Then the joke hit, and my husband gave me a quick kiss before his laughter joined my own.

"Sleeping Beauty—good one," my husband chuckled.

"What do you mean?" I asked, pretending to be offended. "Don't you think I'd make a fantastic beautiful sleeping princess?"

"Yes, dear. Whatever you say, dear."

"Humph."

"So Vanessa, now that I know your humor is intact, what about the rest of you? Do you feel good enough to get out of bed?"

"Don't worry," I said as my husband once again became chivalrous and helped me into a sitting position. "Whatever was wrong with me before, I feel great now. I must have just needed to catch up on my sleep."

Still chuckling, I swung my legs over the side of the bed and stood up. My chuckles halted as my head began to swim and I had to make a quick choice to either sit back down on the edge of the bed or fall to the floor. I chose to sit.

"What's the matter?" asked Tony, concern returning to his face.

"It's nothing really, I just feel a little weak."

"You look as white as a sheet."

"I think its just hunger."

"Well, no wonder," my husband replied, his face once again relaxing, "you have gone at least thirty-six hours without eating. Anyone would be weak."

"I guess I know how to solve this problem," I said with a nod, "I'll eat some breakfast, and everything will be back to normal."

I stood up again, determined to overcome that irritating feeling of weakness. I wanted to reassure my husband that there was nothing to be concerned about. The best way to do that was to hide any feelings of weakness and walk to the kitchen so that I could feed my body the nourishment it craved.

I had only managed to take a few steps away from the bed when I was hit by a tidal wave of queasiness.

A familiar wave of queasiness.

"Oh goodness," I said, stopping dead in my tracks. "I recognize this feeling, and it explains a lot."

"What feeling?' Tony had moved over to stand near me. I think he was readying himself in case he had to catch me if I began to fall to the ground.

"This feeling that the inside of my stomach is about to make a speedy exit."

"You're nauseous? Are you sick?"

"Not sick—pregnant. This is that old, way-too-familiar feeling of morning sickness!"

"Thank goodness. I can handle you pregnant, it's much better than any other sort of illness."

"What do you mean illness? Pregnancy isn't an illness!"

"Now wait a minute. I didn't call it an illness! I said it was much better than an illness!"

"You said 'other' illness. Which implies that you think pregnancy is an illness."

"That's not what I meant."

I looked intently at my husband's face as I tried to discern exactly what he was feeling. I saw a bit of exasperation, a lot of relief, but not even a smidgen of joy.

"Oh no! Tony, don't you want this baby?" As panic began to set in, my voice became higher and higher. By the time I got to the word "baby", only the dogs in the neighborhood could hear the sound of my voice.

"Of course I want another baby," my husband consoled, "I love children, particularly our children. But don't you think you are getting a little ahead of yourself? You don't know for sure you're pregnant. This could just be the flu or something."

"There you go again, calling a pregnancy an illness. It is not an illness, it's a miracle!"

"I know, I know. But it could be the flu."

"I've had three babies," I responded, insulted that he thought I knew my own body so little. "I know the difference between the flu and a baby."

"Okay, okay, don't get offended," he said cautiously, aware that he was on shaky ground, "but why don't you take a pregnancy test just to be sure. It wouldn't hurt."

A pregnancy test was a reasonable request. I also would not mind getting that confirmation. Just for the record—I already knew what the results would be.

"I'll do that," I said as I nodded my head, "as soon as I get dressed. I think I can probably get one from—"

I stopped midsentence, suddenly aware that when one had morning sickness, one should shut one's mouth and run to the bathroom.

Which was exactly what I did.

I was in such a hurry that I neglected to close the bathroom door. As I rinsed my mouth in the sink I noticed—assembled in a little half circle in the hallway—an audience of three of the gloomiest little faces I had ever seen.

What a peculiar sight! Three little bundles of energy, sparks who usually could not stay still for more than three seconds, were sitting perfectly immobile in utter misery. As I continued to rinse my mouth, I wondered what was going on in their little minds.

I did not have long to wonder.

"Are you…" Becca, the eldest and therefore the spokesperson, had risen to her feet and moved over to place her hand on my arm. "Are you…" again she paused.

"Am I what, darling?" I asked, curious to discover what was going on in her head.

Becca looked at me a moment, and then turned to look at her sisters. She seemed to draw courage from their grave little faces, so she turned back to me a continued solemnly, "Are you going to die, Mommy?"

My heart fell to my feet. My little ones were worried I would die, just because I had an upset stomach and had slept overlong? Poor darlings!

"No, sweetie," I said gently as I grabbed Becca and gave her a quick hug, "Mommy's stomach is just a little upset. I'm already feeling better."

"Mommy..." Maddie jumped up and moved closer, "do you want a glass of water before you go back to sleep?"

"No thank you, darling, and I don't think I'll go back to sleep just yet. Don't you think I've slept enough for now?"

"Yes, Mommy, but it's not time for you to get up yet."

"Not time for me to get up?" What was going on in this child's head?

"No, Mommy. You need to go back to sleep until Prince Charming kisses you. Then you get up."

I looked at Maddie and realized that she was perfectly serious. She was not yet of an age where she could differentiate between fact and fiction. In her eyes, she was not pretending I was Sleeping Beauty, I was Sleeping Beauty.

"You are so right, sweetie," I now had my arms wrapped around my second child. "But your dad has already kissed me, and he is my Prince Charming."

The worry on Maddie's face was instantly replaced by a sunny smile. All was now right in Maddie's world.

"How about you, Zoe," I asked, releasing Maddie and turning to my youngest daughter who was sitting alone in the hallway, "are you worried about Mommy?"

With a nod and a sniff, Zoe jumped up and flew into my open arms. After an anaconda hug— good thing she was so little, or I would not have been able to breathe—she gave me a very sweet kiss on my cheek.

"Your breath stinks, Mommy!" was my angel's frank comment.

I had intended to eat a piece of dry toast as soon as possible to calm my stomach, but my daughter's comment changed my mind. I would brush my teeth before going to the kitchen.

Even sick mommies had to be good models. Ruining everyone's appetite with my stinky breath would not set a very good example.

Kids, you had to love them—especially the preschool group. As soon at a thought was born in their little minds, it jumped right out of their mouths. Preschoolers had no concept of filtering. Their honesty was brutal!

⁂

I had dry toast for breakfast, and only dry toast. The morning sickness of my three previous pregnancies had been the virulent kind—I had lost fifteen pounds the first few months of each pregnancy. Not only did all food smell obnoxious to me, but the miniscule amounts I managed to force down tended to hold incredibly precarious positions in my queasy stomach. If the past was any predictor of the future, dry toast was the safest meal—for breakfast, lunch, and dinner.

Whoever first coined the phrase "morning sickness" was an idiot. My guess was that he was a man, a man who could not avoid the evidence of his wife's queasy stomach first thing in the morning, but who went merrily to work as soon as he could. Out of sight, out of mind, would have been his policy. Since he had not seen her distress throughout the rest of day, she had not had any.

Besides, it was all in her mind, anyway. She needed to stop being so weak and have dinner waiting on the table when he got home from a hard day at work.

My guess must be the correct one, or "morning sickness" would not have such a wimpy name. It would instead be called by a more accurate description, like "all day sickness", or "misery months", or "trimester of the volcanic stomach."

I needed to stop thinking about terminology and start focusing on technology, specifically the technology that would tell me if I was really pregnant.

What joys were ahead of me! I could not wait for that speculating look strangers gave in the early months, as they stared at my protruding belly and tried to figure out if I was fat or expecting a child.

After that there would be the delight of the ever-expanding belly, which fit perfectly well into a shirt one day, but stretched it to its limit the very next.

Followed by the pleasure of perfect strangers disregarding my personal bubble to pat my stomach—as if the pregnancy negated normal cultural customs and made me to become public property.

Throughout there would be those ever popular visits to the doctor, where I would be required to assume awkward poses while the doctor poked and prodded.

And bathrooms. Loads and loads of bathrooms.

If I had had any doubts about my pregnant status, the thoughts of the last few moments would have pushed them aside. It was perfectly obvious that the hormones had kicked in full force.

Besides, I knew the difference between normal queasiness and pregnancy queasiness. There was an indefinable something that set it apart.

·ⁱ ·ⁱⁱ ·ⁱ

"Are you sure you feel okay enough to drive?" Tony asked as he walked me to the car ten minutes later.

"I don't know, darling," I teased, suspecting that the show of concern did not go quite far enough for him to actually go to the store to purchase the test for me. "I not sure I feel well enough to drive. Maybe you should go to the store instead."

"Me? You want me to buy the test?" Panic flooded my poor husband's face as he thought of the ordeal.

"Would you please? I think my stomach is too upset for me to drive."

"Well…I could make you more toast. Would you like more toast? I'll go make you more toast."

"I don't want any more toast. I want you to go to the store for me."

"I would, but I would buy the wrong thing." He was perfectly willing to scrunch up his face with worry, but there were limits to his compassion

"I'm not an expert on pregnancy tests either. Just grab the first one you see."

"I…I…I can't."

"Why can't you?"

"I…I have a huge test tomorrow, and I might fail the class if I blow this test."

"You have a test, a huge test?"

"Yes."

"Tomorrow?"

"Yes, and I haven't studied nearly enough."

"So you need to study?"

"Yes. I have a lot of studying to do."

"You can't even take the time to run to the store for one little purchase?"

"Oh no, I shouldn't even be walking you out to the car now. I need to buckle down and start studying. Immediately."

"I see. So do you think, maybe, that I should just not take the pregnancy test?"

"No! You should take the test."

"But I feel sick. And if you don't have time to go get it for me because you have to study—"

"I'll be studying all day, but I bet your stomach calms down soon. You can just go to the store later, when you feel better."

At that, I decided to stop teasing my panic-stricken husband. It was pure cruelty to make him think for even a minute that he would be forced to go out in public and touch any object that could be found in that special "women's things" aisle of the drug store. My husband was a mere man after all.

"You know," I said with a sigh, "I think I'm feeling a little better now. I should be able to go to the store and get the test myself."

"Really?" Tony asked. He looked pretty much like I would expect a man who had just sat down in the electric chair and had been handed a pardon from the governor to look.

"Really, I'm fine, don't worry."

"Well, the girls and I will be waiting for you here."

"Don't forget to study for your big test."

"What? Oh. Yes. I'll get right to that."

Tony opened the door for me, and I got into the car and started it. As I turned to back up, I was struck by the realization that this was a five passenger car, and we were soon to be a six-passenger family.

Not to mention our 900-square-foot apartment.

If there was another baby on the way—I knew deep in my heart there was—we would need to make some major changes. This baby would alter our lives dramatically.

Then again, since the beginning of time every birth of a child has momentarily disrupted the flow of the universe. How else could it be, since each newborn child held the seed of all that was good in humankind, as well as all that was bad?

There was no greater joy, no nobler source of excitement, than the birth of a child.

But there was also no greater responsibility. Each parent must face the challenge of nourishing and guiding all that potential. It was tragic that not every parent stepped up to the plate and took that momentous responsibility seriously.

A twinge in my side pulled me back from the La-La Land of—well, wherever that La-La Land was located—and I realized that the car was in reverse, I was twisted around to look behind me, I was still in my parking space...but I had not even remembered to close the car door.

Yes, the hormones had indeed kicked in.

I took a quick look toward my home, and was pleased to note that Tony was nowhere in sight. He had missed my lapse of focus.

The store was only about half a mile away. It would be more refreshing, and much safer, if I hiked it rather than taking the car. I climbed out of the car, carefully shut and locked the door, and began to walk.

As I neared the store I caught sight of four classmates about to go inside. I hurried to catch up with them to say hello, but I was careful to hide the true purpose for my shopping trip.

These particular friends, the poor deluded fools, were members of a Zero Population Growth group. It was little wonder they were childless and unmarried.

Or could it be they had joined the ZPG *because* they were childless and unmarried?

Either way, early on in our acquaintance each of them had taken it upon herself to lecture me because I had selfishly procreated three times. Each thought she could save the world by bombarding me with statistics that proved that humans were ruining the world because of our ability to reproduce massive numbers of offspring.

The first attacker was the only one who had the opportunity to fully have her say. I spent a full day in shock after her lecture, and then I pulled myself together and did a little research of my own. From that day forth I was prepared with data that countered every statistic the ZPG crowd could dig up.

The four ZPGers eventually admitted defeat. Their statistics were no better than mine, so they simply shut up.

My fear was that a new pregnancy would revive the battle. I did not have the time or the energy to waste on more skirmishes.

I chatted about classes for a few more minutes, said my farewells, and grabbed a shopping basket. A few cheap toys for the girls and toilet paper would provide sufficient cover for my shopping trip, in case anyone was nosey enough to look. I knew from past experience I had several friends just rude enough to peek in my basket and ask questions about its contents.

A pregnancy test in my basket, all alone, plain for any and all to see—I might as well take out a full page ad in the newspaper.

When I had my basket half full of nonessentials, I headed over to THE AISLE. The one that women went through quickly and men avoided like the plague. The place in every drugstore dedicated to embarrassing items necessary only to women.

I reached the aisle just as one of my friends left it. Moving quickly, I located the pregnancy tests and grabbed the one I had seen most often on television commercials. After stuffing it securely under all the items in my basket I moved to another aisle. There I surreptitiously snuck a glance at the package. Fantastic! I had been in luck and grabbed one with the price sticker firmly in place. All the stealth in the world would have been useless if the cashier had asked for a price check over the loud speaker.

I almost lost my nerve when I moved to the front of the store to pay. There was a line at the checkout. Even more horrifying—the most anti-population growth of my classmates was having a hard time deciding what flavor of gum to buy, and the gum rack was located right beside the checkout counter.

If I was unwise enough to get in line, this particular classmate was sure to strike up a conversation and stick around while I made my purchases so that we could enjoy a nice long chat together.

What to do...what to do? I had to keep her from suspecting that I might be pregnant. I could not let her catch sight of the test.

Just as panic was about to set in I remembered the cosmetic counter. It had its own, separate checkout line, which was usually empty.

I zigzagged my way to the side of the store, stopping to look at various harmless items along the way so no one could ascertain my true goal. I felt I was rather good at this covert business, maybe I should consider a career as a private detective, or a spy.

I reached the cosmetics section, and was immediately relieved to find no one in the vicinity except the cashier. Probably because the ZPG crowd rarely wore makeup. I made my purchases in blessed obscurity; unseen and unheard.

As I took the receipt from the cashier I breathed a sigh of relief. The ordeal was over.

Or so I thought; until I reached the door that stood between me and safety.

I could not make myself push the door open.

I just stood there, frozen, rooted to a spot about a foot in front of the closed door.

Why could I not move? What was wrong with me? Why did my hand ignore the command to reach out and touch the door? Why did my feet disregard the instruction to step closer to the closed door?

What was happening? How could a closed door instill in me so much anxiety that it was impossible for my body to move toward it?

Frantically I looked around. I needed a distraction, something that would help me avoid a total meltdown.

Spying a newspaper rack to the right of the door, I sauntered over to it as casually, as if I had not a care in the world. Reading the newspaper would divert my mind, help me calm down, and keep me from looking the fool.

"Oh, no!" I gasped as the headline caught my eye.

On the front page in big bold letters was the name of my best friend. I scanned the article and was shocked to find that Erica had disappeared from campus sometime during the night.

My heart began to beat rapidly, pumping fear throughout my body. What could have happened to my friend?

I grabbed a paper and got back in line to pay. I was so caught up reading the story that I almost did not remember to thank the nice gentleman who held the door open for me as I exited the store.

Erica was missing?

I staggered down the block in a state of shock.

Erica was not the type of girl who hung out with the wrong crowd. She did not do drugs, she was a serious student, and she was not the sort to run off without telling anyone. She had taken multiple self-defense classes and kept her mace and taser with her at all times.

Thoughts of Erica swirled around my head as I walked home...questions of "why" chasing questions of "what" followed by questions of "who." As the questions built up, so did the feeling that my brain was drowning in pea soup style fog. If I did not find answers soon...

As I rounded the block, I could see my husband standing in the living room window watching for my return. As if a fresh sea wind had blown by, the fog engulfing my brain was instantly dissipated, and all thoughts of Erica were whisked away.

Selfish or not, my family had to come first. I could do nothing to help find Erica. I could do quite a lot to allay the fears of my family.

By the time I reached our front porch, Tony had the door opened wide, and the worried look on his face melted my heart.

One step through the doorframe was all it took before I was engulfed in the hugs of my serious-faced children.

I kissed each member of my family, told them there was nothing to worry about, and headed for the bathroom.

This time, I made sure I took the time to firmly close the door.

Chapter 20

"WELL, THAT MAKES IT OFFICIAL," I whispered to my reflection in the mirror, "number four is on the way."

After all the complaints I had heard, all the grumbling that these tests were nearly impossible to read, I had been prepared for a real struggle to understand the results. But whether it was this test in particular, or just me, I found nothing to misinterpret. I was pregnant. The results slapped me in the face, danced a jig, and then glowed in big neon letters.

On a positive note, I now knew that the horrendous nausea that had incapacitated me this morning was caused by the hormones of pregnancy. I had not contracted some mysterious illness.

Positive. Yes. Another child.

I sat down, dazed and shocked, on the edge of the tub. For the fifth time I reread the instructions on the box and looked again at the test—just to make sure I was not making a mistake somewhere. There was no room for doubt. I was pregnant. And flabbergasted.

Please do not misunderstand. I wanted another child, and every fiber of my heart cried out a welcome to this new child. But I was a realist, and I made it a policy to face facts head-on.

My life was once again about to change dramatically. I needed to think, to process the transformations that were about to take place. Fortunately, I was sitting on the edge of the tub in the only room in the entire house where a person could be assured of a little privacy. Now was the perfect time to face the consequences—the good, the bad, the ugly, and the gorgeous.

I would start with the ugly truths and get them out of the way.

First and foremost, a new baby would unquestionably slow down my education. The memories of late nights spent walking a newborn to calm her, extreme fatigue due to lack of sleep, never having a moment I could call my own—all were crystal clear.

As were the benefits of all that walking. A couple of months after the birth of each of my children I became the proud owner of an impressive set of guns—the muscle kind. My newborn munchkins really gave me fantastic workouts! They made the most incredible personal trainers. If I attempted to skip a workout, they wailed. If I tried to eat, they bawled. Even the need for progressively increasing weights was handled by my newborn personal trainers. They simply gained weight at just the perfect rate.

There was no doubt that with all the work required to take care of a newborn, there would be no time or energy left for lab work. Every waking moment would be spent taking care of this tiny person, this little human who would be totally helpless, totally dependent on me. If I was fortunate enough to find a spare minute, I was sure I would want to spend it sleeping. I recalled the massive sleep deficit I had for the first few months with each child.

If I had to think of the ugly, I might as well mull over the expense of another child. Babies are pricey, and I do not just mean the hospital bills. There were diapers, clothing, a new car seat...

The car suddenly loomed large in my thoughts. It had been a good car, maybe even a great one. But it had to go. It only had room for five passengers, and we were about to become a six-passenger family. Buying another car was a must, and a huge expense.

The thought of the car reminded me that Becca had dance lessons I needed to drive her to, which then reminded me that the birth of this child tacked an extra four years of kiddy shuttling to and from classes, school, and friends' houses.

The timing of this child was a bit unfortunate. We were only one year away from having all of our children in school. Scheduling of our college classes would have become exquisitely easier. But now—

I slapped my hand to my head as I looked around the tiny bathroom. How could I have forgotten our 900-square-foot apartment? We were already packed into this place like sardines, with all three girls sharing one bedroom while Tony and I took the other. Exactly where would the poor child sleep? The first few months would be fine, but after that the baby would need some sort of space that could be called his or her own.

Later, when we had solved the biggies like housing and transportation, we would have braces, and presents for friends' birthdays, and shoes, and school supplies, and sports, and driver's education classes, and a college education, and...well, the costs for each child seemed never-ending.

With that quite hefty list of uglies out of the way I could now move on. I would have to address each ugly as it came. Luckily I had other children and knew that the physical stresses would pass. Children learned to sleep through the night and move around on their own at some point or another.

As for the expenses...well, with a little scrimping and a little prayer we would find a way. We would take one step at a time. No need to worry about a college education for a child who was not even old enough to be in diapers yet!

So on to the fun part...the positively gorgeous.

The very first gorgeous obliterated every single negative listed. Who cared about the expense and fatigue? I had the chance once again to experience the miracle of birth! To have the responsibility of a new life growing in me — amazing was an understatement!

This baby, like every baby, had the full potential of humankind sitting on his tiny shoulders. Who knew what this child would grow up to do, how this child might change the world. The possibilities were mind boggling.

On a less grandiose and more personal note, I looked forward to having another member of my family to love.

I so enjoy my children. I could not even count the number of times they have caused me to laugh out loud, often involuntarily. Their antics are priceless! Some of the most engaging characteristics of my children have to do with their ability to entertain.

As a matter of fact, my husband and I have already saved a bundle of money on entertainment costs because of our three children.

Feeling down and need a few laughs? Now playing in the dining room, the lighthearted comedy, *Beauty and the Beach*. An unscripted adaptation of the well-known fairy tale, starring Barbie and friends.

Famished and in need of a break? A visit to the kitchen was sure to hit the spot. High tea was currently being served, a culinary delight consisting of juice, crackers, cheese, carrot sticks, and cookies. Proper dress and manners required for this highly structured royal tea party. Sustenance, snootiness, and sauciness—served with tea.

Bogged down with worries? Gain new perspective on life through the eyes of a distraught child in search of a favorite toy. Join in the adventurous quest for the missing treasure, experience the excruciating emotional pain as the realization that the treasure was truly lost hits home, plumb the depths of tragedy.

Our grown-up worries pale in comparison to the colossal burdens of a child. It's all in the viewpoint.

My husband and I have no real need to leave the house for entertainment. We have masters of the fine arts of the theater living right in our midst. Without a single class or lesson they have managed to be more addicting than my favorite shows on television, more dramatic than the saddest tear-jerker movie, and funnier than all the circus clowns put together.

Entertainment value aside, what I enjoyed most about my children was their sweet nature. One look from those innocent, trusting eyes and my heart melted. I could never deny my children anything, anything at all...unless it was not good for them, or would cause them to become spoiled. I had no intention of raising brats.

Enough introspection. It was time to face the music and inform my family that we needed to make room in our lives for a new addition.

Would the baby be a boy, or a girl? Another girl could be pleasant. Girls were very sweet. But a boy would also be nice, since we did not have one of those. It would be a new experience, and I had heard that every man wanted a son. Did Tony wish for a son?

I was stalling, and I knew it. There was no reason for me to waste energy worrying, or even thinking, about the sex of the baby. Only time would tell. The baby would be whatever the baby would be. I could think and plan and wonder until the cows came home and it would change nothing.

In preparation for facing my family, I pulled my shoulders back and straightened my clothes. It was best to exhibit a tidy demeanor.

Was I ready? No, not quite. First, I needed to rewash my hands and face. I wanted to look composed...and clean.

Was I ready now? I looked at my face in the mirror. Good, I certainly looked normal enough...and clean.

Holding my head high I reached for the doorknob. My hand stopped a mere two inches short of its mark. I ordered my arm to stretch further, but it refused to budge. I pleaded with my left foot to take a step closer to the door, but my left foot did not respond. I begged my right foot to take the step, but I was ignored.

The doorknob stayed just out of reach. I knew I should have been able to reach out, grab the knob, turn it, and go talk to my family. But somehow, no matter how hard I tried, some inner aversion would not let me touch it.

Curious, I attempted to touch the wood of the door. The same aversion that would not allow me to grab the knob also kept me from touching the door.

What a ridiculous situation I found myself in—trapped in the bathroom by my own inhibitions! What kind of hang-up was this? Was I really that concerned about what my family would say about the baby?

After a moments thought, I decided it must be something else. Deep in my heart I knew exactly how my family would react when they found we were to about to add a new member to our family. They would be ecstatic.

Could this be a strange reverse-craving caused by the pregnancy? Instead of a craving for ice cream, I had an aversion to doors.

Come to think of it, this feeling was the same as the one I had felt earlier, at the store.

What an odd symptom. Even though I had read a million baby books, I had never heard of anything quite like this before.

Whatever the cause, I was stuck. The thought of touching the door filled my body with terror. I needed help.

"Tony," I whispered. I wanted to be just loud enough that my husband could hear me, but quiet enough that the girls would not pay attention. I had already frightened them enough with my excessive sleeping; they thought I had become Sleeping Beauty. The little darlings.

"Tony, are you out there? I need help. I can't open the door," I said a bit louder.

"Tony," I yelled, slightly panicked. Where was my husband? Why did he not answer my call?

Frustration made me want to bang on the door, but I still could not touch it. So I did the next best thing. I banged on the wall a few times. I would have kicked it too, but I was afraid I might put a hole right through it, and then we would have to pay to have the wall fixed.

When all the banging and yelling elicited no response, I decided to put my ear to the wall. Nothing. No little girl sounds, no running feet, no giggles, no playing, nothing.

Where did my family go?

Then it hit me. Tony had probably taken the girls out to distract them while I took the pregnancy test. After this morning's fiasco when I neglected to close the door and they had witnessed the full brunt of morning sickness...well, the girls deserved a little distraction.

I had one option and one option only...to wait. My family could not be gone long, Becca needed to get ready for her dance class.

I might as well make myself as comfortable as possible. The side of the tub looked like a reasonable place to sit.

After an hour of so of waiting, I discovered that the tub was made of extremely hard material, and perching on its ledge hurt multiple places of my anatomy. I slid down to the floor, hoping that it would prove more comfortable.

At least I would not die of thirst, or need to run around searching for a bathroom. It was a small comfort, but it would do in a pinch.

A pinch was exactly what I found myself in. One created by my silly inability to open doors. Really, who had ever heard of such a ridiculous pregnancy symptom! Why could I not just crave pickles and ice cream like a normal person?

My heart skipped a beat as I heard the front door slam, and then began to race as footsteps ran down the hall toward me.

I was listening to the sound of salvation so intensely that I jumped and nearly fainted when the runner knocked on the bathroom door.

"Mommy, I gotta go."

"Come on in sweetie," I answered softly, struggling to control my impulse to scream at the top of my lungs.

As the door swung open and I saw my eldest daughter framed in the doorway, I only had one thought.

Freedom at last.

Chapter 21

THE WEEK THAT FOLLOWED WAS the hardest of my entire life. I worked tirelessly to keep my aversion a secret, so tirelessly that I became exhausted! At times I wondered if all the secrecy was worth it, if it might not be better to bite the bullet and call a press conference to share my pregnancy-induced anti-craving for closed doors with the world.

I cringed as I imagined the possible headlines, "College Student Fears Doorknob, Stuck in Bathroom for Hours," or "Open Doors for Pregnant Women, the Baby You Save May be Your Own," or "New Pregnancy Symptom Discovered," or "Pregnant Woman Gives Birth in Classroom, Claims Inability to Open Door as Reason," or

285

maybe "Crazed Pregnant Woman on Loose," or maybe "Woman Kept Prisoner by Unborn Baby."

No, no one outside my immediate family was going to hear a peep about my strange condition.

Oddly enough, this new condition made me love and appreciate my husband even more than before—which was fortunate, since I was often stuck in rooms with him until he chose to open the door and let me out. Among the things I learned about my husband were that he hated to let subjects go until they were fully exhausted; he was physically unable to look away from a football game until the commercial; and his sarcastic sense of humor could bite.

What a clown he turned into! How he enjoyed having a captive audience!

But most important of all was Tony's ability to put aside his humorous antics. As soon he fully understood the gravity of the situation— after I finally got him to believe that this was not an elaborate joke I was trying to pull on him—I had his full support. He instituted a rule within our house that all doors would remain open at all times. He himself was the only person allowed to close doors.

It was not as hard as I had expected it to be, since my daughters had not yet mastered the fine art of closing doors of any kind anyway. Then, when my husband told them the rule was to keep doors open, they showed a hereditary propensity to carry things to the extreme. Not only was every door kept wide open, but so were all cabinets and drawers, backpacks were left unzipped, coats remained unbuttoned, and the lid to the toothpaste disappeared entirely. We became a very open family.

I was safe in my own house. Only my husband closed doors, and only if he felt our conversation needed to be truly private.

There was one room in the house where even I wanted the door closed, provided I could get it open again. My husband found the perfect solution. During a very entertaining ceremony, with much pomp and circumstance, my oldest daughter was promoted from mere daughter to Official Bathroom Door Opener Extraordinaire. She took her duties as OBDOE very seriously.

It only took an hour before we discovered we would need a second ceremony. My other two daughters, who had felt left out, were very excited with their new official titles of OCC (Official Cabinet Closer) and KORD (Keeper of the Refrigerator Door).

I had no intention of letting this aversion get the best of me, so I worked hard every day to overcome it. After a lot of struggle I finally progressed to the point where I could at last touch a partially open door. The real breakthrough occurred when, with a little will-power, I forced myself to open it to the point that I could squeeze through.

Yes, I had now reached a new pinnacle in my life...a partially open door no longer created an impenetrable roadblock to my progress. Success came in many forms!

I would never forget the first time I tackled the bedroom door, a monumental obstacle I was determined to overcome. I took a deep breath and calmly reached out to touch the cool smooth surface, only to find I could not get past an unseen barrier about a foot from the door. Undaunted, I focused harder on my goal and willed my fingers to inch toward their goal. My fingers did not move so much as a millimeter.

Frustrated, I switched my focus to the doorknob, that shining beacon of freedom that represented liberty. I used every fiber of concentration I had available to imagine my hand grabbing the knob and swiftly opening the flimsy little door that stood between me and the rest of the world. I was again unsuccessful.

As my struggles continued, the hope I cherished in my heart was quickly being replaced by a toxic terror that polluted my body and brain with poison. I began to fear I would die in this room, alone and frightened. So real was this fear that my heart began to race, and sweat dripped from my face like I had just completed a 10K marathon.

This feeling of hopelessness, despair, and fright could not be good for the unborn child I was carrying. Was the child now swimming in a sea of misery, poisoned by fear and hopelessness?

That my fear of closed doors was irrational, illogical, and silly only made matters worse. This was not claustrophobia, since I knew that I would never remain trapped in any room in this house for long. My husband had made sure I was protected, all I had to do was raise my voice a little and the OBDOE would immediately open any door for me.

The pounding heart and terror came from the thought that I had let myself down. I had a strong will—I should be able to overcome this fear.

I would overcome this fear. I was not done yet. I had not been raised to be a coward—or to require the constant services of a personal servant. I was an independent woman, able and willing to stand on my own two feet.

I had always been able to open doors for myself in the past. I would not go through the rest of this pregnancy hampered by every closed door, forced to wait for someone to open it for me. I had to find a way to beat this thing on my own.

So I lectured myself about the dangers of feeling sorry for myself and gave myself a little pep talk. Then I began again, determined to succeed.

The breakthrough came about in a surprising manner, and required no superhuman strength or willpower.

After more than an hour spent reaching for an object I could not touch, I was frustrated, tired, and a little teary-eyed. I decided to take a little break, so I simply stood before the partially open door that had proven to be such an effective barrier and listened to the sound of my children joyfully playing in another room. I smiled as I recognized a favorite game of pretend.

Just as I began to relax, reassured by the happy sounds of kids being kids, I heard a crash and a cry of pain from my youngest child. She had stumbled and fallen. My mothering instincts kicked in and I was through the door in a flash.

It was not until I had my child safely cocooned in my arms that I realized I had accomplished my goal. It only took a moment's thought to figure out what had happened.

You see, while I was focused on the problem, represented by the hard surfaces of the door and the knob, I was trapped. But when my concentration waned enough that I no longer noticed the problem but only saw my goal, represented by the soft light shining through the crack in the door, I was free. It only required a shift of focus.

Never again would a partially closed door impede my progress. I was over it. Fully closed doors…well, they were another matter.

It was time for me to return to class, but luckily for me, I attended a university with over forty thousand students, most of whom would not know how to close a door if their life depended on it. All of the main doors into the buildings were ADA compliant, so an elbow to a switch caused the magic of electronics to open those doors. Inside the buildings doors were usually propped open.

For the doors that were not propped, I could rely on the heavy stream of students that flowed throughout the campus. Few doors stayed closed for more than a few minutes.

It was just like the old adage; when one door closes another one opens. I simply had to make sure I was around to take advantage of the door that was opening.

The true test of my ability to overcome this pregnancy-induced obstacle would happen tonight. I had an upcoming deadline for a project that could only be completed in the lab. Tony needed to stay with the kids; Erica was sadly still missing; and my other classmates had already completed the project. No one would be with me to be the official door opener.

I would be on my own. Late at night there would be no constant stream of students, randomly opening doors at the most fortuitous moment.

Not finishing the project was not an option, so it was time to move to the next step and tackle a fully closed door. I could do it, maybe.

If not, I could always sleep on the cold, hard floor of the lab, where all those dirty feet have walked.

Or the cold, hard counter top, which would at least be slightly cleaner.

Or, here was an idea—I could push several stools close, tie their legs together, and create a bed. It would be elevated above the germy floor *and* have a built-in cushion. In the "Best Place to Sleep While Trapped in a Laboratory Overnight

Because You are Unable to Force Yourself to Open the Door" contest, the bed-made-out-of-stools was the undisputed winner!

Of course, I might not need to resort to staying the night. The best solution would be to complete my work and go home to my very own pre-built, soft, clean bed. I could take the Night Shuttle so I would not have to worry about being trapped by a closed car door—the Night Shuttle driver always opened and closed doors. Once home Tony could open the front door for me. He would get up in the middle of the night to do that one little favor for me. I was sure he would not mind. Given the circumstances.

Denny Hall itself presented no problem, since the door to the basement was ADA compliant and had one of those big magic buttons.

Why was it I could not touch a closed door, but I had no problem pushing the big button that activated the mechanism that automatically opened that same door? It made no sense.

So I knew I could get into my house once I got home. I could get home by shuttle and the driver would open the door for me. I could leave Denny Hall via the automatic door.

Which left the lab itself—the real problem.

I would be in the lab alone. No one would be around to open any closed doors. The rules of the lab stated that after nine p.m., all doors must remain closed and locked.

Locking the door was not a problem, because I could lock it before I allowed it to slam shut. It was the unlocking and the opening that concerned me.

The bed-made-out-of-stools idea might be a good one after all. I should stuff a pillow in my backpack just in case, a tiny little pillow that would provide comfort without taking up too much space. Just in case.

Unless, and this was a real stretch, I disregarded the rules and propped the lab door open until I was ready to leave. I was by nature a rule follower. Breaking rules did not come naturally to me, as it did to so many other students.

Surely my first venture into the world of rule breakers would be forgiven, if I were caught. I could not imagine that any university official would want a pregnant woman to remain trapped in a basement all night. Not if a simple bent rule could prevent such an occurrence.

I breathed a sigh of relief when I arrived at the lab just as a class was leaving. The door was propped open wide, just the way I liked it.

I left the door propped open for a full hour after I heard the last student exit the building. Then I searched the room for the biggest, heaviest, widest object I could find. In the back corner, hidden under a pile of old newspapers, I hit pay dirt in the form of a 1953 edition of a dictionary that must have contained every word ever spoken. It was huge, bulky, and would make the perfect

293

door stop. It was time to break a few rules, put aside my fears, and get really get down to work.

⁌   ⁌   ⁌

Done! I looked at my watch and smiled. As I stretched to remove the kink I had gotten from sitting hunched over in one position for too long, I congratulated myself for completing a project in four hours that the professor had warned the class would take at least six.

Two hours saved…two whole, wonderful, precious hours. And I—like any other mother of three small children who was expecting a fourth child—knew exactly how I wanted spend those two valuable hours, sleeping. It was time to get out of Dodge, or at least the lab. My comfy, cozy bed was calling to me, *Sleep, come home to me and sleep.*

I stretched my arms over my head and began to gather and shove my belongings into my backpack. I had just zipped it closed when my actions were halted by a strange sound that had begun to permeate every corner of the room.

The humming noise bothered me not just because it was out of place, but because it was familiar. My conscious brain told me I had never heard it before, while my subconscious hinted at another story.

The memory I was trying to recall was elusive, fuzzy, and insubstantial, just out of reach.

Had I encountered this strange humming noise in a dream?

I knew of nothing natural or man-made that made quite that sound. It had a haunting, echo-like quality that I could not place. I did not understand what would make that sound, and why it would be here in the basement of Denny Hall in the middle of the night.

But maybe, just maybe, I was not really hearing this noise. It might be that the sound had a dream-like quality because that was exactly what it was—a waking dream, a figment of my imagination. After all, if my pregnancy could cause me afraid of closed doors, could it not make me also conjure up strange noises?

This reassuring theory lasted all of a minute and a half, until the sound of footsteps reached my ears. Very real footsteps that could not be a figment of my imagination, and that seemed to be right outside the lab door. Footsteps that sent chills racing up and down my spine.

For the first time, I regretted my decision to prop open the door. I had worked late in Denny Hall often enough that I knew the schedule of the custodial staff like I knew my own. By this time of night they were always long gone. The security staff patrolled outside the buildings, but did not enter them unless they had a specific reason.

Visions raced through my head of terrorists intent on planting bombs, anarchists up to no good, and thugs looking for a victim.

As I stood frozen, immobilized by fear, the sound of footsteps in the hallway changed. It was no longer a small group that had invaded Denny Hall, it was a large crowd.

Could I sneak over to the door and slide my doorstop out of the way before the crowd in the hallway noticed the open door to the lab?

If I closed the door, would that help me, or put me in a worse position? It would certainly hide me from the attention of those in the hall, but would it make my situation better, or worse?

It really depended on the intentions of the invaders. If they were in search of a victim, my best bet was to close the door. But if they were intent on burning down the building, closing the door would be the worst thing I could do.

What to do, what to do?

Chapter 22

HOW IRONIC. I WAS TRAPPED in the basement of a university building in the middle of the night by one of my pet peeves—Indecision. Yes, Indecision with a capital "I." Good old Indecision was an enemy that often lurked around my house waiting to create havoc on my day and wreck my schedule. As a mother of three young children, Indecision was the bane of my existence.

One of my jobs as a parent was to teach my children how to weigh the odds, look at the options, and make a decision. But my children are indecisive creatures, and it was not an easy task.

My husband and I have spent years struggling on a daily basis to guide each child through a plethora of decisions—some important,

297

but many irritatingly insignificant. We had a few successes, but often we were frustrated in our endeavors by the reappearance of Indecision just as we had the child ready to make a choice.

We finally agreed that when it came to the minds of our children, the decision-making process would continue to be a long and arduous process for many years to come. We decided to make a pact that we would refrain from taxing the decision-making muscles of our children if the child was tired, cranky, or in a hurry. Or if we were.

But we all slip up sometimes, and just the previous week as we were getting ready for church I...well...I was not thinking clearly. I made the mistake of asking my youngest child if she would rather wear a blue, green, or white dress.

I broke our rule. My child was not tired or cranky, but we were all in a hurry. We were always in a hurry Sunday mornings. There was never sufficient time to get our family ready for church.

With one thoughtless sentence I transformed my happy three-year-old cherub into a stressed-out little monster. As soon as the words left my mouth I realized the damage I had done. Indecision brought panic, and panic brought tears.

I had no excuses to fall back on. I had broken the rules. It was up to me to short-circuit the storm that had the potential to grow into a hurricane.

Zoe went to church that day dressed in an outfit that was an exact replica of the one worn by her older sister.

I apologized to Becca, who took pride in being fashion forward. It was difficult for a girl to be truly fashion forward if her little sister copied her every outfit.

All these years I had assumed that the one fatal flaw in the characters of my children, that inability to make a decision, had been inherited from someone on my husband's side of the family. How humiliating to discover that I was the culprit, that I possessed the could-not-make-up-my-mind gene, that I had passed it down to my children.

If my children ever got wind of my vacillation, if they learned of my indecisiveness, would they ever trust my judgment again? Would I lose my ability to be an effective mother and mentor?

They were young, and would never understand about the extenuating circumstances, my inability to open closed doors. All they would see was that I had shown weakness, a lot of weakness. They might rationalize that if their mother could not make a simple decision, if their mother caved at the first adversity, why should they be expected to do better?

I would not allow myself to give in to my biggest pet peeve, the one that drove me batty on a daily basis. I could not surrender to the character flaw that made me pull my hair out in frustration.

Could this be yet another aspect of my pregnancy? Was I destined to spend the next few months unable to make decisions? Were the hormones running rampant throughout my body interfering with my ability to think and reason?

Too bad I was adverse to pain—now would be a great time to slap a little sense into myself. But since the thought of self-inflicted pain was extremely disagreeable I did the next best thing. I gave myself a mental pep talk and told myself to get a grip! I would never be able to teach my children that it was best to meet challenges head-on if I ran from this test.

I made a quick list of all the pros and cons and unearthed a surprising discovery. I was more willing to come face to face with terrorists intent on mayhem than I was to spend the night in the lab. Possible danger was no match for sure discomfort.

Decision made, I planned my next moves. I would tiptoe over to the door, put my eye to the crack, and check the hall for intruders.

If the intruders were hanging out in the hallway, I would need to re-examine my options. Which I hoped would not happen, since I really did not want to spend the night in the lab.

I remembered the aches and pains of past pregnancies, and the need for a soft place to sleep.

I also recalled the extreme queasiness that met the morning sun. What a pleasant sight that would be for those students who were first to class.

I had to go home.

Time to be brave, decisive, and adventurous.

Chapter 23

EVERYTHING WAS BLACK. IT WAS as if I were in a tunnel where no sights, sounds, or smells could reach me. A sudden loud noise popped me out of my tunnel, and I became aware of the sound of breathing—my breathing. Warm light hit my closed eyelids, turning them bright red. I took in another breath and detected a faint hint of pine.

Odd. I had no recollection of doing anything that might make me lose consciousness.

The last thing I remembered before regaining my senses was my courageous decision to peek into the janitor's closet to see if the intruders had left a little present for the university. One that would go boom and ruin the day everyone in the vicinity.

One minute I was in the hallway bravely sleuthing, the next I was in a black tunnel.

I started to open my eyes, but hesitated. I was not certain I was ready to face whatever might come next. No one who had a reason to be in the building would accost an unarmed woman in the middle of the night and knock her out cold. Or at least, no one in their right mind, since I suppose it was possible that there were a few crazy folks around with legitimate reasons to be in the building.

Until I had more data, I really did not want to know if I was in the clutches of a group of crazies or terrorists. Not that there was a lot of difference. All terrorists were crazy, although not all crazies were terrorists.

In my best and worst case scenario I was in the hands of people who were one egg short of a dozen. Or maybe even several eggs.

As I lay there trying to figure out what I should do, I realized that something did not quite feel right about the floor. It somehow did not feel solid enough, cold enough, floor-like enough.

Cautiously, I brushed my fingers across surface, relieved to find it smooth and cool to the touch, just as it should be. Emboldened by my success I moved them a few more inches.

Where were the edges of the tiles? The hallway of the Denny Hall basement was tiled.

I needed more information, but I was afraid that too much movement on my part might draw the attention of my captors. I needed other information-gathering mechanisms, ones that I could employ without raising a single finger.

My mind was immediately hit with brainstorm after brainstorm, each gale force wind bringing with it an idea crazier than the last.

It took me several minutes to clean up the mental wreckage left behind by the storms, and I was amazed at how many of the plans were impractical, difficult, and just plain dangerous.

I sifted out the most outlandish plans, those that required the help of armies or helicopters, and tossed them into my mental landfill. It was quite a hefty pile.

Then I filtered out strategies that required the use of tools. Another immense mound joined my imaginary trash heap.

Finally I threw away any tactic that might put me in a dangerous situation.

In the end, I was left with only one stratagem. It required me to lie still, be quiet, and pay attention to my surroundings. I could do that.

My plan had been inspired by an article I had read that stated that when a person lost the use of one sense, the other senses became enhanced. I planned to keep my eyes shut for a while longer, encouraging my other senses to compensate.

It might not immediately get me out of my predicament, but it was a safe alternative to some of the crazy things that had whipped through my head.

Lying here with my eyes closed, I was amazed how much information I could gather while appearing to be unconscious. One of the first things I noticed was the same strange humming noise that had bothered me earlier. Keeping my eyes closed allowed my ears to focus on the sound, and I could tell that something about it had changed. Earlier in the night the sound had had an echo, as if it were emanating from a well. Now the echo was gone and the hum was clear and precise.

I cautiously took in a deep breath. The familiar musty smell of the basement was missing. It was a smell I had grown to love. One that reminded me that the building was a solid piece of history, and that generations of students before me had spent long hours of study within these walls struggling to better themselves, to stuff their heads full of knowledge, to learn what they must so that they could go out into the world and make it a better place.

Fear coursed through my veins as my senses continued to provide me with fresh information. A shift in the air brought the fresh smell of plants, a tropical mixture of flowers and fruit with the slightest touch of the sea.

If I had been standing I might have fainted. Every bit in information my senses brought to me pointed to the same conclusion, every scrap validated the theory that I had tried to keep from forming in my mind—I was no longer in Denny Hall.

I probably was not even in Seattle any longer. The air was wrong, very un-Seattle. It was ion-charged, like the air during a thunderstorm.

I needed to find Toto, because it was clear that I was not in Kansas anymore...and by Kansas I meant Seattle.

There was no doubt about it—I was up a creek without a paddle. I was in over my head. I was on a roof without a ladder. I was...oh, why even try to come up with any more? I was in trouble. I needed to find out where I was, who had me, and what they were planning to do.

I had gone as far as I could with my enhanced-senses plan, now I needed to open my eyes.

Was I ready? Did I have the courage? As soon as I opened my eyes, as soon as my captors discovered I had reentered the land of the living—

My internal dialog halted midstream as my ears caught the sound of a door opening and footsteps entering the room.

"How can she be here again?" a man's voice questioned. His deep voice sounded more frustrated and confused than angry.

My heart began to pound erratically as I realized that these must be my captors—my crazies— and I must be the "she" under discussion. No need to open my eyes just yet, I could just pretend continued unconsciousness and gather more information.

"Well," began a second male voice, clearly that of a younger man. During a pause of about half a minute all I could hear was a light tapping noise. It took all my self-control not to peek.

"Stop tapping that infernal machine and talk to me. Either you know why she is here or you don't. Which is it?"

"Well…," the second voice again hesitated.

"Out with it!" Evident frustration made the man's gruff voice almost into a bark.

"I'm sorry, but I can't explain it," the younger man said calmly, "it just isn't working."

"What have you done?"

"We've shielded her, repeatedly."

"Is that the normal protocol?"

"It is."

"And…"

"She is a curious woman. Each time, she again wandered through the portal."

"Well, shield her again!"

"We can't shield her again, and you might not want to yell. She should be waking up any time now. I'm surprised she hasn't already."

"Fine, I'll lower my voice. So why can't you shield her again? I've read the historical reports. I know there have been a few people who required three or four procedures before it took."

"She has already gone through the process four times."

"Well, do it again!"

"I refuse to do anything so irresponsible."

The silence was so thick you could cut it with a knife. I focused my attention on my breathing. It would not do to let them suspect that I was feigning sleep.

"I don't understand," the older man said, defeat evident in his voice. It was as if he were on a general on a battlefield about to embark on the greatest battle of his life, only he had just discovered that his weapons were mere toys made out of plastic.

"Let me see if I can explain," the younger man's voice assumed a tinge of authority. "You understand what happens with the shielding?"

"I believe I do. A block is put up in front of the memory we don't want the person to remember."

"That's the explanation given to laymen. The actual process is much more complicated, and can be extremely dangerous."

"Dangerous? How?"

"Well...most people think that the human brain is structured like a computer, with specific storage areas for specific data."

"Go on."

"But the human brain is more like the ocean, with currents of data, instead of segments of data."

"Currents?"

"Yes. You see, what we attempt to do with shielding is to place a block in front of a particular current, so that the memory cannot flow."

"Got it."

"But the problem comes because memories can mix together, like water can mix."

"What kinds of problems can this cause?"

"If we make the slightest mistake, if the memory we want to block is mixed with an important memory…"

"You inadvertently block a memory that the person needs?"

"Yes, and we have found that different people have different degrees of mixing."

"And this woman?"

"The 'waters' in her mind seems to mix together to an amazing degree."

"What happened?"

"We should have known after the first shielding that we were going to have a problem. Rarely have I seen such a reaction."

"What was the reaction?"

"She forgot her family."

"Hmmm. Not at all what we want. Were there any repercussions?"

"No. Luckily she was smart enough to hide her lack of memory from her family. At some point the part of the shielding that made her forget her family failed, and her memory came back."

"All of it, even her memory about us?"

"No, that part of the shielding stuck. But the very next time she was near the portal she walked right through."

"Do you have any idea why? The portals are placed in such a way that we should not have random people just wandering through."

"All I can think is that she is a very curious woman. She can't leave a mystery alone."

"And we are a mystery? How does she even know we exist?"

"She doesn't. She just likes to explore the unknown. There is something about our portal that sparks her interest, and she gets curious. She wants to know more."

"So she waltzed right back through. Then what happened?"

"We shielded her a second time and sent her home. But this time, she lost her sense of style."

"That's not so bad. There are a lot of bad dressers out there."

"I misspoke. When it came to clothing, she lost her common sense. She couldn't even figure out how to wear a pair of pants."

There was a moment of silence after this comment, and I could feel my face blush red at the thought of my fashion faux pas. I silently prayed that the two men would continue their conversation and not turn their attention my way. Unconscious people did not blush.

"I see," the older man said thoughtfully, "and did she regain her ability to dress herself?"

"Eventually. But not before her family became concerned that the stress of school had unbalanced her mind."

"But she didn't remember us?"

"No, but she did wander back through our portal."

"I think I'm beginning to see a pattern here. What happened the third time we shielded her?"

"She forgot how to cook. She remembered the rudiments...but again, commonsense flew out the window. For some reason she added cinnamon and sugar to every dish she made. Her children loved it."

"And her husband?"

"Fortunately, he was out of town at the time. She snapped out of it before he returned home."

"So if I counted right, we are up to the fourth time you shielded her. What happened with that shielding?"

"We were desperate for the procedure to work, so this time we hypnotized her first."

"Hypnotized her? Why?"

"Well, it seemed to us that each time we shielded her, we unintentionally shielded a necessary part of her memory. We were fortunate that she always regained access to the part we didn't mean to block."

"Right."

"But each time, she came back to us. She seemed to have a fascination with the portal."

"It seems so."

"So we hypnotized her to have an aversion to the portal. That way she wouldn't come back, no matter what. She would not be able to."

"It sounds like it was a great plan. Why is she here?"

"There is something about her brain we can't predict. We must not have hypnotized her correctly. Instead of an aversion to just the portal, like we wanted, she became afraid of all doors."

"All doors!"

"Yes. You can imagine the hassle."

"I certainly can. But that still doesn't answer my question. If she was afraid of all doors, how did she get through the portal?"

"She taught herself to overcome the aversion. What can I say, she's strong-willed."

"She certainly must be! So let me get this straight. In each instance, the shielding backfired and caused her to lose some important part of herself. And in each instance, she snapped out of it on her own?"

"Yes."

"So what do you predict will happen with the fifth shielding? Will you do anything different?"

"There won't be a fifth shielding."

"What?"

"Have you forgotten the baby?"

"Of course not! How could I?"

"Then maybe you don't realize that each time she left here, she forgot she was pregnant. It is much safer for the baby if the pregnant woman knows she is pregnant."

"I agree, but every time she walked through that portal, she created danger for us."

"Right."

"So what do you suggest we do?"

I found I was holding my breath. I convinced my lungs to relax a bit, so that my breathing would sound a little more normal. I did not want anything to interrupt this conversation.

"First, I want you to understand that this is her fifth time here."

"I can count. I heard what you said. I understand that this is her fifth time. What I don't understand is why you say she should not be shielded again."

"We have never had anyone have a serious negative response to a first shielding."

"Or the fifth, I'll wager."

"You would lose that wager."

"What?"

"The first shielding is like a freebie. No one has ever gotten hurt. But each time we shield someone after that, we run the risk of making them into a vegetable."

"Why? I thought shielding was harmless."

"The human brain can only take so much. Only so many currents of memory can be blocked before the brain shuts down."

"So you are saying she could become a vegetable?"

"Yes, I am."

"What would happen to the baby if she became a vegetable? Would it survive? The baby is the important one, not the mother."

"If she becomes a vegetable, we are lost."

"That makes no sense. She is only a footnote in the history books. It is her children who are important, not her."

"Do you have children?"

"Why yes, I have a girl and a boy. Why?"

"How old are they?"

"Fifteen and twelve."

"Fifteen and twelve. Very impressionable ages. If you died right now, at this moment, do you feel confident that it wouldn't affect your children? Do you feel they would still grow to be exactly the same people regardless of your presence? Does your influence make a difference?"

The older man must have been imaging the life of his children without him, because several moments went by in complete silence.

"Well?" questioned the younger man.

"I get your point."

"We don't need the baby to just survive, we need her to grow and flourish. This woman's children grew up to be who they were partly because of heredity, but partly because of the influence of their parents. Without this woman's help in their upbringing, without her influence, you never know how they would turn out. It might all go bad, like the other time before."

"Other time?"

"Yes, there was one other time when we had a subject like this. When we kept shielding and shielding, but the subject kept returning."

"And how many times was that subject shielded?"

"The total of five."

"Who was the subject?"

"The subject in that case was a man. You probably wouldn't recognize his first name, Alois."

"Should I? Did he play any part in history?"

"Do you recognize the name?"

"No."

"Even with your military background, you don't recall anyone with that name?"

"Alois. Alois. It doesn't ring a bell. What is the last name?"

"Hitler."

"Hitler! As in Adolf Hitler?"

"Alois Hitler was Adolf Hitler's father."

"Good grief! You shielded Adolf Hitler's father five times? How could you?"

"How couldn't we? No matter what we did, he just kept coming back. He was a very curious and, well, let me be truthful, intrusive man."

"But five times? You just told me that shielding someone that many times is extremely dangerous."

"It is, but Alois Hitler was the first subject we had ever had who required that many shieldings. We didn't know there could be a bad effect. What could happen."

"So…what did happen? What effect did it have to shield Hitler's father so many times?"

"According to the history books we keep in the Timeless Room, Adolf Hitler should have only had a minor role in the history books…as an artist. An artist who was also a minor government official, and who stated that he owed his success in his art to the steadying influence of his father."

"And when you shielded his father that fifth time…"

"He did not become a vegetable. Instead, his heart gave out and he died."

"And history changed?"

"History changed radically."

"Then what are we to do?"

"With this woman, we already know she plays a part in history. Without her—"

"What would happen without her?"

"It is unknown. But I truly believe her presence is important for her children, and we want her children to have the childhood they are meant to have."

"So we cannot risk shielding her again?"

"No. We'll have to do something we have never before done."

"That is?"

"We'll have to tell her the truth, and let her go back home unshielded. We'll have to trust her."

Chapter 24

I WAS IN SHOCK. I had to focus every ounce of concentration I could muster to keep my breathing level until the men left the room.

It was fortunate I was already lying down. Otherwise, I was sure I would have fainted.

What was I to believe? Could any part of the conversation I had overheard between the two crazies be true?

It could not be true. I must have been transported to an asylum while unconscious, and I had just overheard a conversation between two of the inmates. They certainly seemed like they were frequent fliers on the La La Land Airline.

Then a horrible thought rocketed into my brain. These men were not inmates, they were my captors. They had too much freedom of movement to be inmates.

But crazy or not, I felt confident that these men were not a part of any terrorist group. Their form of fanaticism had nothing to do with blowing up buildings, or planes, or schools, or anything else.

I found comfort in this thought, since I wanted to keep all my fingers and toes intact. I knew myself well enough that I was sure that if I found this group planting a bomb, I would feel obligated to try to get rid of it.

I was not a hero, I just had a strong sense of...sense of...what would I call that sense? Sense of responsibility toward my fellow man? Moral sense? Sense of patriotism?

None of those quite fit. Maybe sense was the wrong word—it was more like a syndrome. A super hero syndrome that caused me to believe I was obligated to save the world.

Whatever it should be called, it had been with me a long time. Even as a child I constantly stuck my nose where it did not belong—I always had to help those who were being wronged.

An innocent bystander who was blown up by terrorists would qualify as a person being wronged. The slightest chance of stopping such a tragedy would make me want to try.

To save a life, I could suffer the loss of a finger or two. I think. Since I had never been tested, I did not know exactly how much I would be willing to lose to help someone I did not know.

I was glad I would not be tested now.

It was a relief to conclude that this group's brand of craziness was defined less by politics, and more by science fiction.

I read a lot of science fiction, but I had never heard of this particular story my captors were re-enacting. It sounded interesting enough—with time travel, memory shielding, and Hitler's dad—that I thought it was worth a trip to the library after I obtained my release. I had a few questions about the story line, and I was curious about the ending.

Chapter 25

I MAINTAINED MY PRONE POSITION a few more minutes, but frankly, I was bored to tears lying still, faking sleep. It was time for me to rejoin the conscious world; to stop dreaming and start living; to fill my balloon with helium and let it fly; to rev my engine and start the race; to…well, really it was time to stop procrastinating and finally open my eyes!

It was silly to not open them. I was in just as much danger with my eyes closed as I would be with them open. Ignorance really did not provide any protection whatsoever; as a matter of fact, most people were better off armed with a little knowledge.

323

So open my eyes I did. The room, which I was pretty sure I had never seen before, was oddly familiar to me. It was one of the worst cases of déjà vu I had ever experienced.

Or was it déjà vu? Through a fog, I caught a glimpse of a memory...

An elusive memory, that was just out of reach.

It was fuzzy, but I could make out myself sitting at a table.

I was in this room, talking to someone.

This memory had feelings attached. I was comfortable and rested, but confused.

I could see it better now. It was, it was...

I almost had it firmly in my clutches. But at the last moment it slipped away—like a wet bar of soap in the shower. It popped right out of my grasp. It was gone.

Frustrated, I reentered the foggy part of my brain and searched. I could find no trace of the elusive memory.

Maybe I was looking at this the wrong way. Some people think the brain was more like a computer, with memories filed away in their proper segment.

I spent a full hour, sending requests for the memory to my internal computer. I tried using everything I could think of in my requests— pictures, words, smells, and sounds—but with no success. I could not get my personal computer to retrieve the proper data.

As a last-ditch effort, I closed my eyes and attempted to put myself into a self-hypnotic state.

I was concentrating so hard on my breathing that I failed to hear the door open. I was not prepared when I heard a voice call my name.

My heart skipped a beat at the sound of that voice. It sounded so much like the voice of my missing friend, Erica.

I opened my eyes and immediately closed them again. I was not sure if I could deal with hallucinations on top of everything else.

"Open your eyes," the voice gently commanded, "I know you are awake."

Whether the woman knew I was awake or not was irrelevant. I was no longer feigning sleep for my protection, I was avoiding reality.

It was Erica's voice, though I knew deep in my heart that this woman could not be Erica. As soon as I opened my eyes and got a good look at the woman, I would have to admit to myself that the resemblance was just that, a resemblance.

I missed my friend. I was very concerned about her. I wanted to imagine her safe, if only for a few minutes.

"Open your eyes, I want to talk to you," the voice that was so like Erica's again ordered.

Gingerly, I opened one eye. But one eye proved to be insufficient. My other eye popped open to take in the sight before me.

Standing in front of me looking chipper and happy was Erica. There was no doubt about it.

I was ecstatic to find the girl who had made the headlines as a missing person was safe.

325

My arms wanted to reach out and hug this girl who I thought of almost like a sister.

But I was confused. A mere week had passed since that last night Erica and I had worked together in the lab.

Yet somehow, in that one week interim, Erica had changed. If looks were accurate, she was about to give birth any minute.

The next few days were some of the most exciting of my entire life.

It was an archaeologist's dream! I was gaining firsthand experience of a culture from another time, talking to the people, touching the artifacts, breathing the air. I got to really understand how this society worked, what made it tick.

Who cared that I was in the future, and archaeologists typically studied the past. Who cared that I would never be able to write a paper, lecture students, or in any way talk about my findings?

It was amazing.

I was absolutely fascinated to learn that Erica had decided to stay in this world, and that it had only taken her a year to find the man of her dreams, fall in love, get married, and start a family.

Never had I seen her so happy.

It was fortunate that no trace of Erica could be found in the history books, or they would not have let her stay.

Erica told me that she was glad she had not made a mark on our generation. She fit in much better in this era than she ever had in the time she was born into.

I was taken on a tour of the city, and was fascinated by the strange dress of the people. It felt more like a movie set than a city.

It was explained to me that the society was extremely stratified, not by classes but by time. Certain people traveled through time, and they tended to bring back their favorite fashions. It had become popular for people to dress according to the time period they identified with most closely. Whole families, and even communities, would adopt the dress of an era.

But in the city, people mixed. So it was normal to walk down the streets and see medieval friars in conversation with French nobility, or a man in a WWI uniform walking hand-in-hand with a woman dressed in the short skirts of the 1960s.

It certainly made for some interesting combinations.

Personally, I thought some of the people carried the dress-in-the-time-you-felt-most-comfortable-with trend a little too far. I saw one man walking around wearing nothing but a fig leaf. I thought it was a little much. Or, to be more precise, not enough!

I also learned that this part of the world had become super green, literally. Almost every building sported greenery to help fight against pollution.

Everyone was terrified of pollution. So much so that scientists regularly visited other centuries to do clean-up. They stole whatever would be used in the next century to pollute.

At least this explained why copper wiring had disappeared at an alarming rate in my time. It was the work of the DTA—the Department of Temporal Adjustment.

It seemed that in 2113, a discovery will be (was) made that allowed massive amounts of energy to be produced using copper wiring. The result will be (was) massive amounts of pollution.

As I said, I found the whole thing fascinating, and confusing.

I wanted to ask Erica more questions, but she got tired rather easily. She was already almost a week past her due date.

Her husband, on the other hand, was ready and willing to answer all my questions. He was the scientist responsible for maintaining the time portal.

"So, does it work?" I asked him when I returned to the lab from my tour. It was mesmerizing to watch the dance-like precision of the lab workers.

"Does what work?"

"Does your ability to travel through time allow you to help the world get cleaner?" I really was curious, since it had been explained to me that they had to be careful of the changes they made in the past. There had been unintended consequences.

"Slightly. It is an excruciatingly slow process. Since the past does not know what it is doing to the future, they tend to come up with new and better pollutants almost as fast as we take the old ones away."

"So why bother going into the past? Why not just clean up the here and now?"

"It doesn't work. We already tried that."

"When?"

"Well, about a hundred years ago. We knew we had to do something, since most of our children were being born with birth defects. Trees worldwide were dying, and the air had a brownish tint."

"You're kidding! It looks so clean now. So what did you do to?"

"We first tried the old fashioned way. Legislation was passed. Non-profits were created for the sole purpose of cleaning the environment. Scientists were given extra funding to focus their attention on the problem."

"And?"

"And it didn't work. We couldn't get all the countries to buy in. Some countries gained huge profits by disregarding the anti-pollution suggestions. The United States and most of Europe

329

almost went bankrupt trying to follow the rules that fought pollution. Very costly rules."

"But something must have worked. The air is so clear!"

"Our scientists found the solution. With the use of the portals."

"Did it take very long?"

"What you see today is a hundred years' of work. One dangerous chemical at a time has been removed from our history. The problem is that every time one is removed, another has been added back in."

"It sounds frustrating!"

"It is, but it is worth it. Through constant effort, the chemicals released into the environment have became less and less hazardous."

"So your world is cleaner? And how are your children?"

"Beautiful! And well."

"So what now?"

"We've shielded your memory four times already..."

"Four times! I thought I had overheard that. I can't believe this is my fifth time here."

"Well, it is. But this time, we want to try something new."

"Will it hurt?"

"I certainly hope not! We want to enlist your aid. We have decided that our only recourse is to trust that you won't tell a soul about us."

"That is some kind of trust. Can I at least tell my family?"

"Would your family believe you? Or would they think you've gone a little nutty? It is very important to us, your future, that your children become the people they are meant to be. Very important."

"Why is it so important?"

"That's the problem with the shielding. You never remember what I told you before. Your children are important because they invent time travel."

"Good grief! My little munchkins?"

"Your little munchkins."

"So I should—"

"Keep quiet about all this."

"All of it?"

"All of it. It would be safer for us all if you kept every bit of it to yourself."

"If I have to, I have to. So what exactly do you want me to do?"

"Nothing, absolutely nothing. Just go about your business like normal, have a normal life...just don't talk about your trips here."

"And my baby?"

"Your baby will be fine, although she will probably confuse your doctor. Based on your due date, she will be several weeks early. But based on her development, she will be a couple of weeks late."

"Why—"

"You've been here multiple times, and the baby has continued to grow and develop no matter what time you are in."

"Do you know the when my baby will be born?"

"Why certainly!"

"Tell me!"

"No."

"Why not"

"That would spoil the fun."

Chapter 26

I HAD MY BABY SIX weeks before her due date. When I went into labor my doctor was so concerned because she was so premature that he used everything in his arsenal to slow down the labor. Nothing worked.

The confusion on his face when she came out fully formed and weighing 8 lbs., 2 oz. was priceless. He could not understand how a baby born six weeks early could exhibit every sign of being a healthy full-term infant.

But I could. It would remain my little secret.

Erica, true to her sweet self, was concerned about the effect her disappearance would have on her friends and family. She gave me a stack of sealed letters to send to her parents, and the dates I should send them. It looked like I would be running a mail service for the next ten years.

She did not tell me what was in the letters, but whatever the first letter said must have done the trick. About a week after I posted it a small article appeared in the newspapers that said the mystery of the missing college students had been solved satisfactorily by the police, and the family was relieved to find that she was safe and sound.

That was all the general public was to get to know. I hoped the rest of the letters would prove as satisfactory.

I have no regrets about the promises I made to the people of the future. I would restrain my curiosity when I see closed doors; I would not wander through any more time portals; and I would do my utmost to push aside any knowledge about the future I had gleaned.

Which is why I wrote it all down in this diary. My private diary, which no one will ever be allowed to read.

If those silly people of the future think I can just shove this whole, gigantic, fantastic adventure into some dusty corner of my brain and forget about it they must be loony. No one could do that!

But what I can do is keep it safe and private. In these pages, that no one but me will ever get to read.

I'll just have to find a good hiding place so that my husband and children will not be able to find this diary. It would not do for them to learn about my experiences.

Not that they would read it if they found it, anyway. They have better manners than that.

You would think that my knowledge of my children's potential future would change the way I treated them. That I would look at them in awe, since I knew they were going to change the world.

I'll admit that it did happen that way the first few weeks after I returned from the future. I don't know what the kids thought about how I behaved toward them, but they certainly were very quick to take advantage of the kid glove treatment.

After a few weeks of handling them as if they were royalty, I had some sense knocked back into me in the form of a triple temper tantrum. All three of my lovely daughters threw fits, at the same time. Over a doll!

As I sat back and took in the spectacle of my former cherubs acting like little devils, kicking and screaming at the top of their lungs about a piece of plastic, the light of reason began to reassert its presence in the form of my dormant Super Hero Syndrome. Yes, the SHS came to the rescue in the nick of time—before the public got a taste of our particularly loud and obnoxious brand of brat—and before these new behaviors had an opportunity to become habit.

Yes, the SHS is to blame for the reinstitution of corporal punishment meted out to my cherubs-turned-devils. I don't believe that it would be necessary to make a note of the details. Everyone deserves to retain their dignity, especially my children—who were, after all, just being children.

I'm thankful that with the help of the SHS I became more powerful than a toy locomotive, faster than a falling bullet, able to leap screaming children in a single bound.

Otherwise, I might have been responsible for unleashing three terrors on the unsuspecting world.

What kind of super hero would that make me? Not a very good one.

So with my parenting instincts back online, I am ready for whatever is to come.

After a quarter off from school to recuperate from childbirth, I will return to school to finish my degree.

On to the greatest adventure of all time.

Family, marriage, college—LIFE.